Death Be Not Proud

Death Be Not Proud

AND OTHER STORIES

JOHN B. KEANE

THE MERCIER PRESS
DUBLIN and CORK

The Mercier Press
4 Bridge Street, Cork
25 Lower Abbey Street, Dublin 1

© John B. Keane, 1976

ISBN 0 85342 470 5

TO PHYLLIS RYAN

The author and publisher wish to acknowledge that these
stories were previously published in *The Irish Press*, *Woman's
Way*, *Woman's Choice*, Radio Éireann and BBC.

Cahill (1976) Limited, Dublin

CONTENTS

1

Death Be Not Proud

The land meant everything to Mick Henderson. The cardinal rule of his long life was its preservation. Envious neighbours whose own land had become run down through neglect and laziness would have outsiders believe that he loved the land more than he loved his wife and certainly more than he loved his family. This was not so. He had been fond of his wife when he married. He had remained fond of her through storm and calm over the years and even now when the physical aspect of his marriage was becoming something of a memory he treasured her companionship in a way that only long attachment can foster.

He would have been hard put to explain his obsession with the land. His wife understood fully and there were others like himself in the valley who felt as he did. These would be silent, tight-lipped men, not without humour and not given to vindicating or modifying what would seem to be an extraordinary pre-occupation with the soil.

At seventy Mick Henderson found himself in a quandary. Labour was becoming impossible to come by. Factories were shooting up like thistles in the nearby towns and cities. Whatever work-force was available in the area was almost completely absorbed. Even his regular workman had deserted him for lucrative shiftwork and a five-day week. The latter was something of a joke amongst the farming community. All the holdings supported herds of milch cows and during the heavy milking periods these needed constant attention.

Once when endeavouring to hire a workman Mick was asked if he would settle for a five-day week.

'You can have a one-day week in the winter,' Mick had told him, 'but until such time as we have a five-day cow there will be no five-day week.'

He had gone so far as to offer free Sundays during the peak periods and occasional days off for special events but there was no competing with the attractions of the factories. He cut down his herd to a manageable size although he was still heavily in debt from having put three sons and two daughters through boarding schools and colleges. There was another son, Mikey, named after himself, a black sheep of sorts, who disappeared one morning when he was barely sixteen after a vicious row regarding his attitude towards further schooling. That was nearly ten years before. Mick Henderson knew his son's address in England, knew he was doing well as a charge-hand in a Coventry factory, knew enough in fact to make Mikey feel downright uncomfortable if he ever suspected such paternal interest.

The others had no feeling for the land, no concern about it. On his seventieth birthday he had betaken himself to the city to consult with his eldest son, Maurice, who was a solicitor there. After listening carefully for over half an hour Maurice submitted his opinion.

'Your safest and your easiest course,' he said dispassionately, 'is to sell out and live here in Dublin or

Death Be Not Proud

AND OTHER STORIES

JOHN B. KEANE

THE MERCIER PRESS
DUBLIN and CORK

The Mercier Press
4 Bridge Street, Cork
25 Lower Abbey Street, Dublin 1

© John B. Keane, 1976

ISBN 0 85342 470 5

TO PHYLLIS RYAN

The author and publisher wish to acknowledge that these
stories were previously published in *The Irish Press*, *Woman's
Way*, *Woman's Choice*, Radio Éireann and BBC.

Cahill (1976) Limited, Dublin

CONTENTS

if city life has no appeal for you there is nothing to prevent you from buying a comfortable house in the country. The money you would make from the sale would clear your debts and leave you with more than sufficient to ensure a comfortable life for mother and yourself until the end of your days.'

His second son, Eddie, was a dentist. Married with two children, he operated from a small surgery attached to his home in the suburbs. Late as it was when Tom called he found Eddie up to his eyes in work. Very late that night they sat round the sitting room fire and talked about the land. It was impossible not to like Eddie and his wife but they had little to offer by way of a solution. They also felt that selling the land would be the best way out.

It was the third son, Martin, a civil servant, who supplied the obvious answer. Mick had a job finding his house in the sprawling, estate-cluttered northside of the metropolis. Snugly seated in the back seat of a taxi he passed row after row of newly-erected, two-storied houses. After numerous enquiries they eventually discovered the estate. Another search and they located the house. It stood amid hundreds of others which looked exactly alike.

'How in the name of God does anyone live here?' he had asked undiplomatically when Martin and his wife met him at the door.

'You get used to it,' Martin said enjoying his father's innate rustic perplexity.

In spite of his first impression he was pleasantly surprised by the interior of the house. It had a heartening spaciousness in contrast to what he had expected.

'You have a fine home Martin,' he announced by

way of conciliation.

'It's only a few hundred yards from the school,' Martin's wife said, 'and that's what really matters.'

After the usual preliminaries Mick settled down to the business of outlining his problems. Martin and his wife listened sympathetically while he explained about the new factories and the scarcity of labour.

'The last thing I want to do is sell it,' he finished.

'The logical thing as far as I can see is to bring Mikey back from Coventry,' Martin suggested.

'Will he want to come back?' Mick asked.

'I have no doubt that he will,' Martin assured him.

Mick Henderson considered this for some time. It was a thought that had always been at the back of his head. All he needed was someone, other than himself, to suggest it. He was aware that Martin and Mikey were as close as brothers could be despite the distance that separated them. In age there was hardly a year between them. It was to be expected, therefore, that Martin would put forward a strong case for the youngest brother. Mick Henderson decided that he would find out how forceful Martin's advocacy might be.

'That's all very fine,' he said disinterestedly, 'but has he the feel for the land?'

'Why wouldn't he?' Martin hastened to reply, 'he's your son isn't he?'

'You're my son and you have no feel for it. Neither have Maurice or Eddie.'

'Look,' Martin pleaded, 'Mikey is different. He's only good with his hands. He was a hopeless scholar. If you had kept him at home when he kicked off the traces that first time he'd know it all now and you wouldn't be worrying about labour.'

' 'Tis easy be wise after the event,' Mick Henderson said. He suspected that Mikey might have the true feeling for the land but there was no way he could be certain. He resolved to probe further.

'What guarantee have I that he won't flog the farm as soon as I pass on?' he asked.

'That's a chance you'll have to take but let me tell you this. Mikey is hardly likely to flog it when it's going to be his livelihood. You know as well as I that he knew how to handle livestock. That time before he ran away he had no objection to working on the farm. What he objected to was school.'

'Agreed,' Mick Henderson returned, 'but there's many a young lad will volunteer for anything to escape school.'

'I happen to know,' Martin's tone was really serious now, 'that if he doesn't come home this year he won't come home at all.'

'Did he say this?'

'Yes.'

'Then I suppose I had better contact him. What if he says no?'

'That's one thing he won't say,' Martin assured him. After this conversation Mick Henderson had no doubt in his mind that Martin and Mikey had discussed the latter's position in depth. On his way home by train he had ample time to think. His one fear was that the land might be sold after his death but this would happen anyway if Mikey refused to come home. He remembered when the farm had been signed over to him by his own father. It had been a bright May morning close on forty years before. He had no idea what his father's business in the neighbouring town might be when he instructed him to tackle the black mare to the family trap. By mid-day he was the legal owner of the land. He had in no way pressurised his father although he had dropped hints that he was thinking of getting married. It was somewhat different in his case. The true feeling for the land was there. His father knew this, knew that the green pastures to which he had devoted the best years of his life would be safe for another generation. It was so important that Mikey have this feeling for the acres which would shortly be under his care. Mick Henderson knew everything there was to be known about the land. Over the years he had discovered its idiosyncrasies and failings and learned painstakingly how to turn deficiencies into advantages. The land had its own unique characteristics, its own vague, imperceptible contours, its inexplicable portions of soft and hard, wet and dry, barren and lush.

On the surface the fields were like any other in the district but he knew better. His father had been a source of constant help as he endeavoured to discover the true lie of the land. Now that he knew all there was to be known it was high time the knowledge was passed on. He would announce his decision to his wife Julia as soon as he got home. She would be pleased. He was aware that she secretly pined after her youngest son although, like all mothers, she became somewhat resigned to his absence as time went by.

The proper thing for me to do, Mick thought, is to impress upon him without seeming to do so the value of well-treated land. I will show him that while human life is to be valued more than anything else, that which sustains it should be valued no less. I will pass over and my wife will pass over but the land will remain. We are only passing through, mere tenants at best. The land will be there forever to nurture my seed and the seed of my seed. Somehow he would try to get these feelings through to Mikey. If the genuine consciousness was there this would be no problem. If Mikey did not fully respond all would not be lost. At least he would not sell and the land would be saved. If one generation failed to throw up a man with love for the land the next generation was sure to compensate. Who could tell but he might live to see a grandson blessed with the appropriate and peculiar disposition so difficult to define.

Mikey Henderson arrived home during the second week of spring. The roadside hedgebanks were bright with clusters of early primroses and along the sides of the avenue leading to the old farmhouse were healthy clumps of daffodils and irises in various stages of flower. It was a good time to come home. During the first months he made many mistakes but Mick was not slow to notice that he never made the same mistake a second time. He was uncannily adept with all sorts of machinery. He understood cattle and most important of all he knew how to husband his strength. He fitted perfectly into the pattern of things.

Mick watched his progress with the keenest interest. Who knew but some evening he might see Mikey with his hands on his hips surveying the sheen of a freshly-ploughed tillage field or shading his eyes against a summer sun on the headland of a meadow ripe for cutting.

With the coming of summer the new green grass, luscious and fleecy, returned to the fields. The hedge-rows no longer bare hosted a thousand songbirds and the first of the long herbage took the naked look from the broad meadows.

The meadows would prove to be the chief of Mikey's problems that first summer. It wasn't a particularly good year for growth. The new crops were light and late and to crown the general misfortune of the farming community there was no labour available when the outlook was favourable for harvesting. The weather too was unkind. To say the least it was inconsistent. Fine days were few and far between and rarely succeeded each other. During this time came the worst calamity that could possibly befall. Julia Henderson took ill and had to be removed to hospital. All thoughts of harvesting had to be abandoned until she recovered.

It was two weeks before she was released. She had undergone a mild coronary. Her doctor warned that unless she cut down considerably in her everyday work there would be a recurrence. After her short stay in the hospital she felt refreshed and the tiredness which had nagged her for so long seemed to have disappeared altogether. She herself declared that she felt twenty years younger and insisted in shouldering her full quota of chores. A young girl was found locally to help her. She agreed to stay until the schools reopened in September. Outwardly, at any rate, Julia Henderson seemed very much rejuvenated. She looked the picture of health and there was none of the breathlessness which she so often endured before her visit to hospital.

There was a general air of excitement all over the district when the weather changed for the better. Despite the fact that there was no immediate prospect of labour Mick and Mikey Henderson decided to make an all-out assault on the uncut meadows. All day they followed each other on two tractors. In their wake the tall grass fell in long parallel swathes. Julia and the girl brought their meals to the meadow. There was no tarrying for small-talk afterwards. As soon as they had eaten they mounted the cumbersome machines. The onslaught lasted until the first faint stars appeared in the late evening sky. The moment they finished they headed straight for the local pub. It wasn't that they especially needed a drink. It was the only place where they were likely to recruit labour. They were partly successful. It was first necessary to invest in several rounds of drink and to exhibit an interest in the welfare of likely prospects that was tantamount to fawning. This, with the offer of almost double the normal wage, was responsible for the extraction of three promises. Both Mick and Mikey were well aware that the trio in question were not exactly the cream of the crop. They would be late and they would put no great strain on themselves but they were labourers and if the weather held the produce of the combined meadows might be saved at the end of three days.

For most of the first day they turned and then tossed the freshly mown swathes. Late in the afternoon they made it up into wind-rows in preparation for the following day's cocking. This completed they broke off. That night the Hendersons listened avidly to the weather forecast. The prospects were still good. Mick and Mikey rose with the dawn. First the cows had to be milked. Then the milk had to be cooled and transported to the creamery. After that it was straight to the meadow. Everything else was secondary. The labourers arrived at ten o'clock and then the business of cocking commenced. First the crisp hay had to be gathered by the tractor-drawn, iron-toothed rake. Mikey attended to this particular function. He worked furiously supplying the needs of the cock-makers who worked in pairs. When the supply exceeded the demand he would jump from the tractor and shoulder huge pikefuls of hay to the base of the developing cock. This was the hardest part of haymaking. One by one, slowly and painfully, the cocks went up until by the end of the second day half the entire crop was safe. The third day followed the same pattern as the second. The mid-day meal was brought to the meadow by Julia Henderson and the girl. On the third day Julia came alone. The girl had not showed up. Enquiry revealed that she had been at a dance the night before and was unable to get out of bed. Julia was not unprepared. She arrived at the meadow shortly after noon, just as the sky was under-going a murky suffusion in the southwest. If rain was to come this would be the direction from which it would threaten. After the meal one of the labourers announced that he was unable to continue because of a stomach ailment. Mick guessed that the pace was not to his liking. The same man had shown himself to be somewhat of a shirker from the beginning. Mikey had heard him derogatorily remarking to one of his colleagues that if he was to die he wouldn't like it to be for a farmer.

Despite her husband's protestations Julia insisted in falling in by his side. They worked together, silent-ly, at a corner of the meadow far removed from the other pair. Julia Henderson was the ideal farmer's wife. Always she had been by her husband's side when the need was there. Of solid farming stock herself, she was aware of her obligations although these had often ranged from milking the entire herd to deputising at weddings and funerals. This was the unwritten law when labour was not to be had.

Now and then Mick would glance anxiously to the west and south where the ominous turgescence of massing clouds was slowly enveloping the otherwise clear sky. By his own reckoning he estimated that there were three, maybe four good hours left. Given that much time all the hay would undoubtedly be saved. He redoubled his own efforts and then without warning of any kind Julia Henderson heaved a massive, choking sigh. Mick stood helpless and appalled while she attempted to restrain with clutching fingers the terrible upheaval in her chest. Then just as suddenly her hands fell listlessly to her sides and she fell backwards noiselessly in a crumpled heap. Urgently Mick Henderson bent and whispered an act of contrition into her ear. There was no disputing the fact that she was dead. He stretched her legs gently and folded her hands across her bosom.

Then he sat by her side awaiting the arrival of Mikey with the next rake of hay. The young man sensed that something was wrong. He dismounted slowly from the tractor and read the news in his father's face. He knelt by his mother's side and kissed her on the lips and forehead. He smoothed back the hair from her face and lifted her head so that he could rest it on the pillow of hay. Then he rose and looked at the sky.

'Let's get on with it,' he said. At first Mick Henderson looked at him uncomprehendingly. Then the logic of it dawned on him.

'What about the two?' he asked, pointing to where

the labourers were building a cock at the other end of the meadow.

'What they don't know won't trouble them,' said Mikey dismissing the question. Slowly his father rose. Already Mikey was adding to the half-made cock. Instinctively his father followed his example.

Before departing for another rake-up Mikey laid a hand on his father's shoulder.

'She would understand,' he said. 'I don't have to tell you that. When the job is done we'll take her indoors. Then I'll go for a priest.'

So saying he mounted the machine and in a matter of seconds was again raking the ever-decreasing windrows. Mick Henderson cast a glance at his dead wife and then his eyes followed his youngest son. Beyond doubt here was a man with a sound sense of values, a man with a true feel for the land.

2

The Reek

The bog was a mixture of browns and greys, grey
where the sun had bleached the exposed turf banks
and the misshapen reeks of yesteryear which stood
along the margin of the roadway. In the moonlight
the grey turned to silver but the brown remained
sombre even when stars danced and the heavens
seemed on fire. When the weather was fine the bog
was my playground. Every goat-path, boghole and
goose-nest was as familiar to me as the lanes and
streets of the nearby town where I lived. I knew the
titles of the turf banks and the names of the reek
owners. I knew the sod depth of every bank and the
quagmires where asses and ponies sank to their
haunches. This was because I spent most of the
summer days with two ancient relatives who lived in a
tiny thatched house on the edge of the bog. They
were brothers. Their names were Mister Chamberlain
and Sir Stafford Cripps. These, of course, were not
their real names. Rather were they soubriquets
invented by the locals on account of the resemblance
the pair bore to the British politicians Neville Chamberlain and Stafford Cripps. The Second World War
was well under way when I discovered the bog and
there was an abundance of Rommells, Montys and
McArthurs so christened because of forecasts they

might have made regarding the outcome of the war or because of certain characteristics relating to the famous generals.

Mr Chamberlain was the older of the two brothers. He was lean as a whippet, bald as a coot and reticent to the point of muteness. Sir Stafford on the other hand was as talkative as he was outgoing. Both were on the old age pension. It was Sir Stafford who tackled the ass and went to town on Fridays to cash the pension vouchers. Mr Chamberlain would not demean himself with such mundane matters and only went to town on Sundays to attend Mass. The pair got on famously. Sometimes there were disagreements but these were shortlived. I remember one such. It was early September. The turf was harvested and new reeks were beginning to appear daily on the roadway. The brothers had earlier cut, futted and re-futted* two sleans** of turf and this stood now in donkey stoolins in the bog on the heather-covered turf bank which had supplied them with turf for generations. It would have to be transported from the bank to the roadway where it would be built into a reek.

Mid-August to mid-September was the recognised time for drawing out. The passages to the turf banks were dry and firm but later they might be rendered impassable by heavy rains. When this happened the turf remained in the bog until the late spring of the following year and the owners had to make do with the remains of old reeks and occasional sacks laboriously drawn on their backs from the stranded stoolins.

* Futting—making wet turf into small heaps; re-futting—making partly dried turf into larger heaps.
** What three men would cut in a day.

'It's time,' Mr Chamberlain announced as we sat on the low wall which fronted the house.

'And I say it's not time,' Sir Stafford countered.

'And why so do you say that?' Mr Chamberlain asked, 'when I say otherwise.'

'I say that,' said Sir Stafford, 'because the man on Hanafin's wireless made a forecast of rain.'

'And what do he know?' Mr Chamberlain asked derisively, 'that couldn't tell one end of this bog from the other no more nor the ass.'

'He knows plenty,' Sir Stafford persisted.

'There will be no rain tomorrow,' Mr Chamberlain spoke with finality. 'The wind is from the right point and there's heating in it and if there's heating in it then by all the laws the sun will be along after the wind.'

To give confirmation to his belief he raised his head and turned his thin, sensitive nose into the wind. I did likewise. The sea was less than five miles distant as the crow flies and sometimes there was a tang of salt in the air. Other times, especially after high tides, there would be a strong fragrance of sea wrack. Often there was the unmistakable odour of decay but it was always possible for a man of experience and judgement to smell out any rain that might be likely to move inland in the course of time.

'There's no rain in that, no rain at all.' So saying Mr Chamberlain rose unsteadily from his seat and sauntered down the roadway towards the passage which led to the turf bank. He had aged more during this summer than he had in all the years since I knew him. He still walked erectly if somewhat irresolutely. There were hints of debilitation in all his steps.

'There's a stagger to him,' Stafford Cripps whispered. I knew what this meant. A stagger was taken to mean that a man was nearing his end, maybe not immediately nor for a considerable time. It was a telling factor, however, from which there was no reprieve.

Later that evening I was invited to participate in the drawing out. I was to be in charge of transport. Cripps was to be posted on the turf bank where he would assist in the filling of the ass rails. Mr Chamberlain was designated reek maker. He had somewhat of a reputation in this field and it would have been unthinkable to have invested him with a less onerous task.

The following day broke bright and clear. There was little or no wind but the air was crisp and cool. The sky was free of cloud and it looked as if the day would be a fine one. Mr Chamberlain had been correct in his forecast for as the morning wore on and the sun climbed higher in the sky it grew distinctly warmer. Each time I heeled the ass cart and emptied a fresh load Mr Chamberlain nodded his appreciation but made no attempt to start building the reek. He merely indicated where he wanted the cart heeled. He knew exactly what he was doing of course. Earlier he had counted the donkey stoolins and made an estimate of the space he would need to contain the entire harvest. He measured his ground with even paces and then with boot lengths for exactitude until a rectangular base was plotted. I had seen him make reeks before. There was no more meticulous builder in the bog. This time he seemed to be more fastidious than ever. He weighed the turf sods with greater care and occasionally he placed a particularly large and well-shaped brick to one side. These would be used later in the clamping.

All morning we worked and as we did the September sun ascended the cloudless heavens. For every step it took upwards the reek took another. At noon we broke for food. This had been painstakingly prepared by the brothers. Mr Chamberlain had lighted a fire during one of my journeys to the turf bank. Atop it sat a kettle of boiling water, a continuous jet of steam shooting from its shapely spout. Wrapped in white muslin was a sizeable wedge of boiled bacon and in another cloth was a pound or so of fresh cheese. There was also a loaf of homemade bread and a solid slab of butter. As soon as the tea was drawn we set about eating. In between mouthfuls Sir Stafford would make a pronouncement.

'There is no sauce like bog air.'

I was too pre-occupied to comment one way or the other.

'Plain food is the best food,' from Sir Stafford again. It went on like this until we had eaten and drank our fill. Then we sat back and relaxed awhile. This was the best part of the day. Other men who were occupied as we were came to join us in order to debate the course of the war. Mingled scents of heather and woodbine imposed themselves fleetingly over the pedestrian odours of the roadway. There was time to savour the sunlit beauty of the bogland while the men spoke on and on of important happenings. Endlessly larks rose carolling from hidden haunts in the heather. The air was clear as far as the eye could see. The little haze there was had long since been burned up by the hot sun. The talk now dwelt on the subject of townspeople.

'I have seen them,' Sir Stafford was saying, 'and

they racking their hair before futting the turf. I have seen them and they wearing low shoes only fit for dancing and they trying to operate a slean.'

Here Mr Chamberlain made one of his very rare contributions to the proceedings.

'I seen the first of the turf-cutting townies at the start of the war,' he said. 'They came in droves when the coal got scarce. I seen strange things but I never before seen the likes of these men. They had bread with meat in the middle of it. You could only see the edge of the meat. The rest was covered by bread above and below. There is no way you could inveigle me to eat meat I couldn't see.'

'It must be sandwiches you're talking about,' Sir Stafford put in.

'The very thing. The very thing indeed. That was the name given to them.'

The talk wore on. It was of times gone by when men worked for coppers and promises and often turned over in their beds at night in an effort to dispel the hollow growling of hunger in empty stomachs. They spoke of spailpins* and labourers who worked from dawn till dark and who had nothing at all to show for their labours in the end, nothing but stooped backs and strained limbs. They spoke of the immeasurable value of book-learning as the one true avenue of escape from drudgery and expressed regrets for the way they had neglected their books in favour of youthful dalliance.

'A schoolmaster now,' someone said, 'he earns a sovereign a day and he don't bend his back.'

'No wonder they're cracked,' Sir Stafford com-

---

* Itinerant farm-workers.

mented, 'money like that would go to any man's head.'

Elsewhere the fate of the world was being decided. Far away in Cairo, Churchill and Roosevelt were meeting with Chiang Kai Shek and in sourthern Italy fierce battles were raging as the Allies endeavoured to advance northwards. We sat drowsily in the lee of the reek grateful for the warm sunshine. The conversation started to flag with the realisation that the time had come to resume work. Later there would be another break for what was known as 'the evening tay'. This consisted of a panny of tea and a slice or two of bread and butter. It was generally a hurried affair at which no time was wasted. There was still some talk but the conversation had lost much of its sparkle. I was despatched in search of the donkey. He had not ventured far. There was an abundance of good grass and wild clover at hand on the margins of the roadway. He allowed himself to be recaptured without resistance as though he knew instinctively that the day was far from being down and there was no point in prolonging his legal recess. I tackled him to the cart without difficulty and in a short while we were working as a unit once more. The pace had quickened as if by agreement although not a word passed between us. There was an urgency to the work now. The pressure would have to be maintained if we were to finish by evening. After 'the evening tay' the old men seemed to grow tired. So did I but it would never do to give the impression that one was unable to pull one's weight. The pace was relentless now but no quarter was asked or given. It would not be too long before the last of the stoolins was on the roadway. It was heartening to see the decrease in their number.

The reek was really taking shape now, assuming that peculiar symmetry with which only a country-man could invest it. There was something here above and beyond blueprints and drawing boards. There was an instinctive insight into the secret shape of the land itself and into this was fitted unobstructively the dark contours of the reek. Instead of standing out it fitted in like a patch into a quilt. I noticed too that it did not run in a precise parallel line with the roadway. Its strongest shoulder better buttressed than the others stood in the face of the prevailing south-westerly wind. Immense knowledge about the peculiar tantrums and exact route of this wind was essential if the reek was to survive the vicissitudes of winter and any reek, no matter how large, was, after all, only as strong as its weakest point. From time to time Mr Chamberlain would walk slowly round its base searching for inadequacies. Often too he would remove himself from the immediate vicinity of the reek and survey it with a critical eye from a distance. He observed it from every angle and from every posture. One moment he would be standing on the tips of his toes and the next he would be lying prone. He inspected it from his haunches and he went so far as to kneel in the centre of the roadway to determine if the upward inclination was gradual enough. Nothing was left to chance. Never before had he been so finical. As the evening wore on he grew somewhat irritable but this passed when the reek reached a certain stage in its development.

Sod by sod, foot by foot it rose to its smoothly-tapering roof until the last ass-load had been deposited on the roadway. All that was left on the turf bank was a carpet of dust and tiny cadhrawns.* Sir Stafford

* Broken sods of turf.

and I untackled the ass. At once he rolled over and
over on the dusty roadway, braying ecstatically.
When he had rolled his fill he flicked his hind legs
defiantly and cantered down a narrow causeway
where a green patch of good grass advertised itself.
The reek was finished except for a few final touches.
The clamping was impeccable. Hardly the width of a
grass blade divided sod from sod. Sir Stafford now
took a turn around it, pausing to inspect a particularly
impressive piece of cornering. With the aid of the ass-
cart Mr Chamberlain mounted the reek and sat astride
its roof. I stood by with a gabhail* of assorted sods.
Occasionally there would be a surgical extension of
his hand and I would tender a sod. He might or might
not accept it, favouring another of different size or
shape. It seemed to me that he was overdoing it. Now
with hindsight I know that he was merely a thorough
and conscientious craftsman who selected sods and
parts of sods the way a poet might select words or
phrases essential to the immaculate completion of the
work in hand.

Also the finished work would be submitted for
critical analysis although it would be true to say that
the most just and impartial critics of all would be the
north-easterly and south-westerly winds. These were
the lads who wouldn't be long pinpointing the flaws.
The accredited critics came that very evening. These
were accomplished reekers themselves. All the reviews
were favourable with the exception of the usual
carper or two whose own reeks could never stand up
to penetrating criticism.

'That won't be knocked aisy,' one white-haired on-
looker essayed.

* Armful.

'That,' said Sir Stafford Cripps pointedly, 'won't be knocked at all.'

The days passed. Autumn went its way in a flurry of russets and winter appeared, unexpected as always but predictably harsh and cold with mighty storms that ranted and raged across the countryside. The reek was not found wanting under the onslaught. It was its maker who was to prove suspect. In January he contracted a heavy cold and because he would accept advice from nobody and stay indoors like a sensible fellow he developed pneumonia and had to be removed to hospital. His condition weakened and one spring morning when the last of the wild geese were winging their way northward he died in his sleep. Shortly after Mr Chamberlain's demise Sir Stafford was smitten by influenza but the neighbours, fearful lest he should be swept away like his brother, maintained a constant vigil and by the middle of March he was on his feet once more, hale and hearty. The reek stood for the remainder of that year without interference. Sir Stafford made do with old turf which lay in a shed at the rear of the cottage. When the season for turf-cutting was under way he hired three young men from the locality to cut a brace of sleans. The reek he left untouched. His decision was not questioned. Artistically it was the best designed and most shapely fabrication of its kind to have been constructed on the roadway for generations. During its third year there was considerable shrinkage but such was the character of the design in the original structure that there was still no unevenness nor was there the slightest evidence of depression from end to end. Now denuded of its original brown by the years of wind and rain, its bleached exterior gave the impression that it had been frosted all over. On clear nights, under an unshrouded moon, it seemed as if it were a great rampart of silver.

Then of a gusty March evening a large band of travelling people appeared at the entrance to the bog. They liked what they saw. They were impressed by the green of the cutaway and if it was a faded green itself the ponies, horses and asses of which the train was mainly comprised were anything but choosy. Down the road they came in three multicoloured, horse-drawn caravans, flanked and trailed by a motley assortment of the most heterogeneous mongrels imaginable. It was a swift-moving but silent caravan. Its occupants, animal and human, were feeling their way. The faces of the menfolk who led the caravan horses were blue with cold. Their noses ran freely. From time to time they would press a finger against one side and expel the rheumy contents of the free nostril with snorts and grunts. As they approached the reek a flock of children suddenly appeared from the interior of the caravans and started to play games on the roadway, contriving, at the same time, to stay in front of the three caravans. When all had passed it was plain to be seen that the reek would never be the same again. There were gaping black holes and cavities along the side nearest to the roadway. Sir Stafford had never taken his eyes from the passing train. Still he had been caught napping by the children's diversions. He knew from long experience that a search of the caravans would reveal nothing. The stolen turf would be instantly and secretively jettisoned at the first sign of danger. Sir Stafford was furious. The reek was now scarred and ulcerous and prey to rain and storm. It would collapse completely in a matter of weeks particularly since it was now certain that further inroads would be made into its already gutted side.

Night came. The fires of the travellers burned brightly in the deep of the bog. Sir Stafford sensed that they would stay awhile, in all probability till the end of April. The reek would stand no chance.

He had looked upon it as a monument to the late Mr Chamberlain. He foresaw a time when it would have naturally and gracefully disintegrated just like its maker but he had never allowed for the intolerable rape of that afternoon. He knew exactly what must be done. In the cottage hearth he built a great fire of heavy black sods. When the coals glowed red he transferred them to a tin bucket and made straight for the reek. The wind was from the east but it was dry and crisp. He selected a favourable spot and withdrew several sods from the base. These he replaced with the glowing coals. For the freshening breeze it was a labour of love to achieve the rest.

3

The Hanging

There is no sight so grotesque or pathetic as the dangling frame of a hanged man. It is an affront to the form of human symmetry. There is no parody so wretched and when Billy Fitz and John Murphy first saw Denny Bruder's body hanging from the cross-beam in Looney's shed they were bemused for some moments by the almost comic presentation of slack hands and slanted head. From the church nearby, as if by arrangement, came the muted tolling of the Angelus bell.

Billy moved first. He touched the hanging foot nearest him and when nothing happened he pushed it gingerly with his palm. The body unexpectedly started to gyrate slowly. The screams of the boys were simultaneous. They ran terrified from the shed.

Denny Bruder had first come to the village about five years before. He was a motor mechanic by trade. He took a lease of Looney's shed and in a short while built a reputation as an efficient man who knew all there was to be known about motor cars. You could not call him morose. Glum would be a more fitting word. He was gentle with children and he never resented their curiosity. He was not the best of mixers and mostly he was to be seen alone going for walks or visiting the cinema where pictures where shown every other night.

In the beginning he was never known to enter a public house and he showed little interest in the local girls but this could have been because they showed little interest in him. He was not the handsomest of men. He was medium-sized with a rather bulbous nose and thick lips. However, he was far from being repulsive. His was a dour sort of face. Older women in the village described it as homely. In time people came to accept him as part of the local scene.

Shortly after Denny Bruder's arrival Imogen Furey invested in a second-hand car. Imogen was the wife of Jack Furey the cattle-jobber. Jack already had a car but, as Imogen told anybody who might be prepared to listen, he was away from home so often at cattle fairs all over the country that they might as well not have a car at all. While Jack was away Imogen would visit his fields outside the village to count the cattle and to see if any wandering animals had broken down fences or forced entry. She would do this in all kinds of weather and since the fields were the best part of a mile from the village she was often in receipt of a dis-comfiting drenching and this, in addition to the time wasted, was one of the chief reasons why she felt the need of the car. There were two children, both girls, but these were away at boarding school for most of the year.

The car was an old model and if it burned more than its quota of oil it suited Imogen's needs nicely. When it broke down one evening as she was returning from counting the cattle she sent for Denny Bruder who towed it to his shed. It transpired that the fan belt was broken. There was nothing else the matter.

While Denny was installing a new belt Imogen suggested that he give the car a complete overhaul. She left it in his care and late the following afternoon he delivered it to her door. She was surprised at the reasonableness of his fee.

Thereafter they became good friends and he took a personal interest in the behaviour of the car.

Midway through his second year Denny Bruder invested in some up-to-date garage equipment. This improved his business considerably and in his third year he found himself with more money than he actually needed. He looked about for a safe spot to invest it.

It was Imogen Furey who solved his problem. Envious neighbours were fond of saying that she knew everything about everybody. By this they inferred that she knew more than was good for her. Uncharitably they would hint that if she paid more time to her own business and less to the business of others she would be better off. This, of course, was a paradox. Imogen Furey was an eminently successful woman by any standards. Her husband was reputed to be the wealthiest man in the village. Her home had every conceivable amenity. She dressed well and was a leading figure on local committees. Her children were boarded at one of the most exclusive schools in the country. On the surface, at any rate, hers was the sort of thoroughly satisfying existence which was bound to provoke resentment and jealousy.

When Denny Bruder confided to her that he had money to spare she asked for time to consider his situation. It was her experience that house property or land were the safest means of ensuring a profitable return from investment. On the outskirts of the

village was a two-storied house in relatively good
condition. It had been on the market for some years
but because its owner was asking too exorbitant a
price it went unsold. She informed Denny that she
was convinced the house could be bought for the sum
originally asked. After an interval of three years she
explained that the price was not in the least exorbitant
by prevailing values.

Denny bought the house, handed notice to his
landlady and moved in. For months he was rarely
seen in public. After work he would spend most of
his time indoors redecorating the rooms and generally
restoring the woodwork, ceilings and anything else he
found in disrepair. When he had finished indoors he
started on the outside. It was early in spring when he
started on the neglected garden which faced the roadway. He planted shrubs and trees and showed an
excellent sense of taste in his selections.

He painted the housefront and windows with
delicately contrasting shades. By late spring the job
was completed. He was more than satisfied with his
handiwork. He decided to sit back and await develop-
ments. All through the summer he confidently
expected a proposal or suggestion of marriage through
some medium from whatever candidates were
available. The house was his chief bait. It was much
admired by the villagers as was the garden although it
was still in a rudimentary state. He worked hard and
which was more important he was seen to work hard.
He bought new clothes and invested in a small comfortable car. The months of summer wore on and
when the trees began to shed the first autumn leaves
he found himself still with an empty house. He was
puzzled. He knew he was no Lothario but he was

also aware that there were many happily married men in the village far uglier and less well-off than he.

He started to visit the public houses. He never drank more than a glass or two of beer. He became friendly with some of the barmaids but that was as far as it went. He went to dances in the village hall and sometimes to neighbouring towns when the bigger, better-known bands included these in their itineraries. He never danced. He often tried but the girls he fancied were snapped up before he could get off his mark. Consequently he spent most of his time standing with other male onlookers at the rear of the hall.

That winter was one of the most miserable he ever spent. He missed the company of the other lodgers in his old digs. The house was unbearably lonely. To crown his misfortune he was smitten by a heavy dose of influenza. He was three days in his bed before anybody showed sufficient interest in his whereabouts to pay a visit to the house. His friend Imogen Furey eventually called. He thrust a muffled head from one of the uppermost windows and told her hoarsely that he was ill. At her bidding he dropped the key to the door at her feet. She was back in less than half an hour with a jug of hot chicken broth. She called again and again until he was fit to resume work.

At Christmas, to repay her kindness, he bought her a present of the most expensive perfume available. The Fureys, to give them their due, knew a decent man when they met one. At Jack's bidding, Imogen invited Denny to a meal one of the nights during Christmas. Afterwards they sat in front of the sitting room fire drinking a special punch compounded by

Imogen.   The heat of the fire and the whiskey to
which he was unused had the effect of totally loosen-
ing Denny's tongue. In a short while he had unfolded
his tale of woe, confessing his loneliness and explaining his most pressing need.

The Fureys were moved first to concern and then
to pity. At a late hour that night Jack Furey drove
Denny home. In bed later on he asked his wife if
there was anything she could do.

'He's a likely fellow,' Jack said, 'and by the cut of
him I don't think he'd blackguard a girl.'

'He's no Romeo,' Imogen pointed out.

'Romeo's don't always make the best husbands,'
Jack countered. Before she slept she promised she
would look into it.

'I'll have to think of who's available,' she said
thoughtfully. Jack Furey knew his wife.

'You'll come up with something,' he announced
sleepily. Through the spring Denny planted more
shrubs and blooms. At his garage he worked hard. He
had, by now, acquired more than a local reputation
and motorists from neighbouring towns would
patronise him occasionally. He took to dealing in
second-hand cars and was soon making more than he
ever dreamed possible. He bought a better car and
went about more. On Saint Patrick's night he was
invited to a party at Fureys. There were other people
present. One of these was a girl from the nearby hill
country. Her name was Nuala Odell. She was auburn-
haired and although exceedingly pale of feature was
nevertheless quite an attractive girl in her late twenties.
She was an indrawn, reserved sort. There had been
talk that she had been seriously let down once by a
neighbouring farmer but this was discounted as

immaterial since almost everybody is subject to some sort of let-down at one time or another, the only difference being that there is never much revelation of these reverses by those who are at the receiving end.

Towards midnight all present gathered round the piano in the Furey sitting-room. Denny Bruder surprised everybody by proving himself to be the proprietor of a very fine baritone voice. The evening was a success. At Imogen Furey's suggestion Denny asked Nora Odell if he might call and take her out some time. She agreed and they settled upon a date. Unfortunately, it was a blustery, rainy night. For want of something better to do Denny asked her if she would like to see the interior of his house. At first she was reluctant but he seemed so genuinely put out that she relented.

After a tour of the bedrooms he asked her if she would like to hear some records. He injected life into the sitting-room fire and chose a selection of Strauss waltzes. The evening was a happy one. She often came to the house after that.

Once he invited her for a meal. He prepared it himself. The main course consisted of curried chicken with the faintest echo of garlic for which she did not exactly care. Otherwise it was a first class meal. Denny explained that during his school holidays he used to help his mother in the kitchen of the hotel where she worked as a cook during the summer. He was an excellent cook and she would seize eagerly upon his invitations to dine in the house. Knowing her dislike of garlic he never used it when she was joining him for a meal. As the months went by Denny Bruder began to fall inextricably in love with Nora Odell. He never told her so. He was content to bide his time and wait for a suitable opportunity. Summer came and on Sundays they would motor to the seaside. Sometimes he would take her father and mother. He was now a constant caller at the Odell home. The senior Odells liked him and Nora's brothers respected him. He was one of the best mechanics for miles and a chap never knew when he might be obliged to visit him.

One fine Sunday in August the pair sat on the grass at the end of a peaceful headland overlooking the sea. Beneath them the incoming tide was noiseless and the flat unbroken surface of the sea like a sheet of silver. Overhead the sun shone from a blue sky. Suddenly Denny Bruder placed an arm around Nora Odell's shoulder.

'I'd love if you married me,' he said.

'Would you,' she asked turning and looking at him directly.

'You know very well I would,' he told her.

'Kiss me,' Nora said. He kissed her awkwardly. After the kiss she took his hand and led him to the shore where the small waves broke listlessly at their feet.

'I'll have to tell my parents,' she said, 'and you will have to speak to my father, ask for my hand if you know what I mean.'

'That will be no bother,' Denny assured her.

'I'm sure he'll be pleased,' she said, as if she had known all along that their marriage was inevitable. Denny Bruder was elated. Without taking off his shoes he ran in the water up to his knees and shouted to the heavens.

'I'm going to be married,' he called out. 'I'm going to be married to Nora Odell.'

They became engaged a fortnight later and a date

was set for the wedding. Neither approved of long engagements and so it was that they decided upon the first Saturday of October. In early September, however, they were to be separated for a longish period. Nora's sister Bridie who was married in Wolverhampton was due to have her third child about this time. She wrote to Nora asking her to come and housekeep for her husband and two children.

Denny drove her to Rosslare which was the port most convenient. As he kissed her goodbye he suddenly realised how utterly empty his future would be without her. She had given his life a new meaning. He was, in fact, a different person since meeting her. People had told him so. It was expected she would be gone for a fortnight. This would allow her a week to prepare for the wedding upon her return home.

During her absence Denny spent every second night visiting the cinema. He always occupied the same seat in the balcony. One night a woman called Angela Fell, the wife of a local shopkeeper, happened to be seated next to him. Midway through the film she suddenly said, 'Oh, oh.' She said it loudly so that her voice carried to the corners of the balcony. Then she left her seat and occupied another at the end of the last row. After the show there was much conjecture. Several different reasons were put forward to justify the uncharacteristic behaviour of Angela Fell. Those who sat nearest Denny Bruder spoke from a position of authority. A young man who sat directly behind Mrs Fell said that Denny was seen to suddenly lift his hand when she uttered the exclamation already described. As to the exact location of the hand prior to its being lifted, he was heard to say, 'where the hell do you think it was?'

By implication this meant that Denny Bruder's hand was placed on an area of Angela Fell's anatomy which might best be described as out of bounds. There were some who flatly refused to believe this. There were others who refused to believe otherwise. Nobody thought of asking Angela Fell. If anybody had I'm certain they dismissed the thought at once. Of all the women in the village she was the least communicative and the sharpest-tongued.

After this incident Denny Bruder was a marked man. People in his vicinity on the balcony would be paying more attention to him than to the screen. Denny had no idea idea he was under observation. A week passed and a teenage girl from the nearby countryside arrived late at the cinema. She fumbled her way to a vacant seat next to Denny Bruder. Couples nudged each other in anticipation. Nothing happened till near the end of the film. Then she left her seat and went outside. There was no longer any doubt in the minds of the villagers.

Some were filled with pity, others with indignation. Imogen Furey found herself in a dilemma. It was she who introduced Nora Odell to Denny. Clearly she would have to do something. One night in bed she asked Jack if he was asleep. He had been away for several days buying calves in the western counties and had earlier retired to bed. Jack Furey was awake. Painfully Imogen related the details of what had transpired in the cinema.

'What am I to do?' she asked.

'Leave well alone,' Jack Furey advised her, 'marriage will knock all that sort of thing out of him.'

'I feel responsible,' Imogen persisted. Jack lay silent. He could feel sympathy for Denny Bruder. He remembered what it was to be lonely, to be so sick with desire that little was beyond contemplation. Essentially he was a tolerant man who was prepared to go out of his way to make allowances.

'I once caught a girl by the knee in the cinema,' he said trying to make light of the matter.

'But you knew her,' Imogen replied.

'I thought I knew her,' Jack Furey said, 'she was no damned good.' Imogen knuckled him playfully on the side of the face.

'It's no laughing matter,' she said seriously, 'I wish to God it was.'

They spoke far into the night. At Jack's suggestion she agreed to do or say nothing until Nora came home. Shortly before her return Nora received two anonymous letters. The day before her actual departure she received a telegram from her older brother which stated coldly that he would be meeting her at Rosslare. She had been prepared to discount the two letters until she read the telegram.

It had been agreed that Denny Bruder would meet her. If her family saw fit to change the arrangement there must be something afoot. Both brothers were waiting when she disembarked. There and then they made her pen a letter to Denny acquainting him of a charge of mind on her part. At first she refused point blank but when they threatened to deal with Denny themselves she reluctantly agreed. She would have liked to hear his side of the story. Family was family however and in the end where else was a person to fall back. She succeeded in convincing herself that she was doing the correct thing. In the days that followed Denny Bruder called repeatedly at the Odell farmhouse. He refused to stop calling even when the older brother appeared at the front door one evening with a shotgun in his hands. In the end both brothers dealt him a severe beating.

After this he concealed himself for a time. It was when word of the beating reached the Furey household that Imogen decided to act. Jack had left early that morning. Before his departure he asked Imogen to pay a visit to Nora Odell.

'If either of them two brothers so much as looks at you sideways I won't like it and you can tell 'em so.'

Imogen nodded. As soon as Jack had gone she made out a shopping list. Shortly before noon she betook herself to Fell's grocery. Mick Fell carefully scrutinised her order which was a substantial one.

'I'd like a word with Angela while you're getting those ready,' Imogen said.

'Of course,' Mick Fell agreed. 'Go straight through.'

Imogen followed a narrow passageway into a tiny kitchen. It was a suffocating place with a gleaming hot Stanley range dominating the entire scene from one corner. Angela was bent over a small table chopping meat.

'I hope I haven't come at a bad time,' Imogen announced. Without a word Angela strode past her towards the shop. Imogen could hear her voice plainly.

'I thought I told you I didn't want to see anybody while I was working. What sort of Goddamned nit are you anyway?'

'Look at the size of the order she's given me,' Mick Fell replied defensively.

'I don't care if she gave you herself,' Angela screamed at him. 'I don't want people collaring me in that hellhole.'

'What do you want of me?' she asked with hands

on hips when she returned.

'Simply this,' Imogen answered tonelessly, 'what did Denny Bruder do to you at the cinema?'

'You have a blasted neck you have,' Angela hit out.

'His hopes of marriage are wrecked,' Imogen forestalled her. 'Tell me what really happened. I promise you no one else will ever know.'

'Get out of here,' Angela advanced a step. Imogen refused to give ground.

'I'm not leaving this kitchen till you tell me,' she declared. 'A man's whole future depends on what you say to me this morning. I'm asking you as one mother to another if Denny Bruder molested you in any way that night at the pictures. If he is innocent you have a duty to perform. If not say so and I'll walk out of here this instant.'

'I have nothing to say to you,' Angela returned. 'Please leave now.' Imogen took a step in the direction of the shop but turned finally and faced Angela squarely.

'If this gets into court,' she said, 'and it well may, you won't get off so lightly.'

The veneer of hard independence faded from Angela's face.

'Court,' she echoed stupidly.

'Yes. Court,' Imogen pressed her advantage. 'That's where they take people who destroy a person's character.'

'I've destroyed nobody's character. I never put a hard word on the man.'

'That may be but you never put a good word on him either.' They stood facing each other. From the shop came the voices of other customers. There was laughter when Mick Fell passed a wry remark. Angela crossed to the table where she resumed her chopping. She spoke over her shoulder.

'He did nothing to me,' she said. 'I left my seat because there was a smell of garlic. When he belched I found it overpowering so I went to another seat.'

'You might have said so before this,' Imogen said accusingly. In the shop she collected her groceries. She resolved to go to Odells that afternoon. First she would see Denny Bruder. Not for the first time she marvelled at the unnatural reticence of women like Angela Fell. Involuntarily she shuddered when she thought of the evil begat by the silence of such people.

As she crossed the roadway to her home the Angelus rang. She blessed herself as did others who were on the streets. Between the peals she could hear the distant cries of children.

4

A Tale of Two Furs

Jack Murphy was a sportsman. By this I mean that it was no trouble at all to him to disappear for a week should there be a succession of sporting events coinciding with a full wallet and a disposition to travel.

He owned a prosperous business and had an excellent wife who always tried to make allowances for him.

He also had a sister-in-law who was forever trying to come between the couple. Jack's was a childless marriage and after fifteen years of 'constant endeavour', as he was fond of putting it, there still seemed to be no likelihood of an addition to the family.

The sister-in-law had come to live with them not long after her husband died. Unkind people intimated that she nagged him to death while others held that he drank himself to death to be free of her.

To give him his due Jack Murphy tolerated her. He never let her feel that she might be an outsider and even his worst enemies were prepared to compliment him on that score. He listened to what she had to say with attentiveness. He would nod politely now and again as she rattled on but he never once indicated by word or gesture whether he agreed with her or not.

Jack's wife Kitty was always expansive in her

gratitude to her husband. She was well aware that nobody else would endure Margaretta for so long. She told him so frequently and Jack, because he loved his wife, would always say; 'ah 'tis a thing of nothing Kitty girl. Where else would she go but to her own?'

From the day he quit his teens and inherited the family business Jack always owned a greyhound or two. Like most greyhound owners he was always patiently waiting for that exceptionally good one to turn up. Sometimes he bred a middling dog or bitch but none had come near equalling any local track records not to mind breaking one. He persevered. He brought good pups and he mated his brood bitches with the best dogs money could buy. For years he had mixed luck. The most promising pups never lived up to expectations but he was in some way compensated when an average dog ran above himself and won the occasional good race.

Then when he least expected it he found himself, one season, with a truly talented bitch. She ran unbeaten in her first five starts and qualified, with little difficulty, for the final of an important sweepstake in Ballybunion.

He trained her for the event as he would any other of his charges and she responded by reaching the height of her form at the proper time. At this stage in her career she was well known. Sportswriters in the national dailies and evening papers predicted a bright future. Like the true doggy man he was Jack Murphy kept his mind to himself. He had high hopes but it would never do to divulge these. The prospect of a big let-down in the long term was always on the cards. As the day of the sweepstake final drew near he was tempted to consult local experts but on the advice of his vetinary he decided to trust to the bitch's natural talents.

On the morning of the big event Jack took his car to the garage and had it greased and cleaned. As he drove back to his home friends and neighbours stood in their doorways and wished him good luck for the night. He acknowledged each and every salute. Somehow he felt that a new responsibility had been thrust upon him. He was possessed of the natural fatalism of all greyhound fanciers but now for the first time he realised that his fellow townsfolk had entrusted him with the onerous task of improving the town's image. Many would be making the journey later that evening to cheer the bitch to victory but Jack was the captain so to speak. He was the very spearhead of the assault.

At home in the kitchen he kissed his wife goodbye. She held him longer than was normal for her. She knew that this was one of the most important occasions in his whole life. Finally she released him and from the folds of her purse withdrew a small bottle. It was partly filled with blessed water which a thoughtful neighbour had brought back from Lourdes.

She allowed a few drops to spill over her fingertips. This she applied to his forehead making the sign of the cross as she did so. She sprinkled the remainder of the water on the bitch. At this stage Margaretta entered the kitchen. Jack knew she would be incapable of wishing him good luck. It was not in her make-up.

'I'll be back some time tonight,' he told his wife, 'or, if not, I'll be here early tomorrow.'

'We all know the words of that song,' the sister-in-law announced to nobody in particular.

'Now, now,' said Kitty, 'that will do you. 'Twould

be more in your line to wish him luck.'

'Luck is the grace of God,' Margaretta retorted sharply. Jack refused to be drawn into the argument.

'You can get Timmy Kelliher to walk the other dogs,' he told his wife. 'Tell him I'll fix up with him tomorrow night.'

Saying not another word he led the dog from the kitchen. He had already removed the cushions from the back seat of the car and covered the floor with a good depth of fresh straw.

'You and me,' he confided to the wide-awake hound, 'will show the lot of 'em a thing or two tonight.' Then he drove off, not heeding now the God-speeds and the waving hands. He was gone but seconds from the kitchen when the sisters had it hot and heavy between them.

'God knows when we'll see him again,' Margaretta spouted, 'it could be days and it could be weeks and then again he might take it into his napper to come back no more. I wouldn't put it past him now that he has the broad road between him and his home.'

'He said he'd be back tonight,' Kitty replied testily, 'and back he'll be.'

'So you say,' said Margaretta, 'but I expect the likes of that when I see it before me.'

'It's none of your business anyway,' Kitty cut her short. 'He's the boss of this house and I don't know where you get the right to criticise him.'

'Oh you needn't tell me who's the boss here,' Margaretta shouted back. 'I know my place. I've been put there often enough.'

The argument wore itself out after awhile but nothing was settled. There was always the danger that it would flare up again.

Ballybunion track was crowded for the feature event of the night, the sweepstake final. The bitch was quoted liberally enough but her price shortened as Jack's friends and neighbours began to arrive. Eventually she was installed a firm favourite at five to four. Jack had been fortunate to get her at fours as soon as the prices went on the boards. He had on twenty-five pounds which meant that he stood to win a hundred pounds in addition to the two hundred and fifty pounds stake money should the bitch cross the line first.

As before all big events there was a sudden silence when the field of six were placed in their respective boxes. The tension mounted as the hare whistled up to the traps and when the dogs broke there was a mighty cheer, each of six contingents shouting for its fancy. The bitch broke well and was second as they came round the first bend.

At the second bend she was third and at the third she was in exactly the same place. Now the roars of the crowd were intensified and women could be heard screaming as the dogs entered the straight.

It was here the bitch showed her real talent. She saw an opening next to the rails, took it like a flash and with it the lead for the first time. She won comfortably. From all sides Jack was pummelled and patted by well-wishers. Supporters fought with each other to shake his hand. Jack said little. The one phrase he kept repeating to nobody in particular was 'What did I tell you? What did I tell you?'

He kept saying this over and over until his admirers departed to draw their money from the bookies.

An hour after the race Jack was entrenched in the corner of a public house lounge with a large number

of friends seated protectively around him. At his feet
sat the bitch. Under his seat was the trophy, a solid
silver cup with the figures of six greyhounds inscribed
around its middle. In his wallet was the money he had
collected from the bookmaker. Also there was the
cheque for two hundred and fifty pounds from the
sweepstake. The cup had been filled and re-filled with
brandy and champagne.

Jack Murphy felt good. He had never felt so good
before. In his hand was a glass of whiskey. He dipped
his fingers in the glass and rubbed them against the
bitch's mouth. Her reaction was to lift her head and
look around wide-eyed at the strange faces. All were
loud in praise of her performance.

'What did I tell you?' Jack Murphy said. 'What did
I tell you?'

A tall figure entered the lounge and a hush fell.
People nodded respectfully and drifted aside as he
moved towards Jack and the sitting hound.

This was   Mister McKechnick the English buyer.
He was as well known on Irish dog tracks as he was
on English ones. He was known to be a decent man
and consequently he was admired and respected
wherever he went. He had a good name as a buyer. It
was said of him that he never looked for bargains. He
always paid what a dog was worth, no more and no
less.

He beckoned to the barman.

'Fill a drink for the house,' he said quietly. When
his bidding was done all present drank his health.
Then Jack Murphy rose from his seat. He was a trifle
unsteady but he was far from being drunk.

'Fill them up again,' he said to the barman.

'You have a class bitch there sir,' McKechnick complimented him.

'Thank you sir,' Jack returned. The two men chatted amiably while those within earshot respectfully withdrew. Business was business and nobody wished to stand in the way of a fair deal.

'What would you say she's worth?' McKechnick asked out of the blue.

'You're too sudden for me,' Jack answered. 'I would have to think that one over for a while.'

'Put some sort of estimate on her,' McKechnick urged. Jack pursed his lips and scratched his head. He looked at the bitch and he looked at McKechnick. He looked at the floor and he looked at the ceiling. He looked at the serious, expectant faces ranged around the lounge and yet he was reluctant to fix a price. He realised that McKechnick was not a dawdler. Rather he was a busy man with little time on his hands.

'I would say sir,' said Jack in his most earnest fashion, 'that she's worth every penny of twelve hundred quid.'

'What you say to nine hundred?' the Englishman asked with a smile.

'I would say eleven hundred,' Jack responded with another smile.

'It looks rather like a thousand then, don't it?' McKechnick said with a hearty laugh.

'It do indeed,' Jack answered with another laugh. McKechnick extended his hand and Jack took it in his. There was a handclap from the crowd.

'I'll give you my cheque,' McKechnick whispered, 'when things quieten down a little.'

Jack nodded agreement. McKechnick beckoned to a small, moustached man at the door.

'My man will take charge of her now,' he said. As

the bitch was being led away Jack suddenly bent down and impulsively flung his arms round her.

'Goodbye my little darling,' he said with tears in his eyes. 'Goodbye and good luck to you.'

At McKechnick's suggestion Jack accompanied him to his hotel. In the residents' lounge the Englishman handed over the cheque. Jack took a ten pound note from his wallet and thrust it into McKechnick's pocket by way of a luck penny. After that they had several drinks.

'You'll be my guest for the night of course,' McKechnick suggested. Jack had no objection. At twelve the Englishman announced that he was about to retire.

'I'm going to Limerick Races tomorrow,' he explained, 'and I don't want a hangover for the day.'

'I'm bound for those very same races,' Jack revealed, 'so I think I'll hit the sack too.'

In Limerick they fared well. During the two days of the races they backed several winners. McKechnick had good connections and the information he received proved most valuable. At night they would do the round of the city's pubs, joining in sing-songs and making new friends. On the final night there were several in the party. They had a hectic time between dancing and singing. Bottle after bottle of champagne was drank. At midnight McKechnick announced that he proposed to withdraw on the grounds that he intended travelling to the Curragh Races on the morrow. He asked Jack if he would care to accompany him. On the spur of the moment Jack agreed.

Quite a large party left Limerick for the Curragh the following morning. Jack rode with McKechnick, a titled lady who owned several racehorses, a bookmaker and two unattached, middle-aged ladies, friends of the titled lady.

Their good luck held at the Curragh. They had a golden rule about daytime drinking. Under no circumstances was anybody to touch a drop until five-thirty in the afternoon. McKechnick had a theory that betting and drinking did not go hand in hand. They had bets on four races. They won on three of these and only lost one.

McKechnick declared more than once that Jack had brought them good luck. At five-thirty they repaired to the Grandstand bar where they proceeded to drink gins and tonics. After an hour the party was a merry one.

At six-thirty the titled lady got on the 'phone to a Dublin theatre and booked seats for the night's performance of a play which, she told Jack, had been favourably reviewed in all the dailies of the previous Tuesday. Jack slept soundly throughout the performance. He was loud in his praise after the final curtain had come down.

He remembered little after that. The night passed in a haze. During a meal in one of the city's more celebrated hotels he fell fast asleep. When he woke up again he found himself in strange surroundings. He was in a comfortable bed in a bright, fully carpeted room. There was a chambermaid, dressed all in white, shaking his shoulder gently.

'They said I was to call you not later than half past eleven sir,' the chambermaid informed him.

'Who told you?' Jack asked.

'Your friends sir, It's Sunday and the last Mass is at twelve. I've brought you some tea. I'll leave it here.'

She carefully placed the tray of tea things on a

chair near the bed. Then she left the room quietly.
Painfully Jack raised his head from the pillows. More
painfully still he eased himself from the bed. He
dressed slowly as though his body was covered with
sores and needed to be treated with the utmost gentle-
ness. He found his way downstairs and thence to the
church.

Mass went by like a dream. It gave him all he could
do to rouse himself at its conclusion. He struggled
back to the hotel, went directly upstairs and straight
to bed.

The next time he woke he felt refreshed. He located
his clothes and went through the pockets. His money
was intact. He lay back on the bed glad that it had
not been stolen. Then for the first time in days he
remembered his wife and as soon as he thought of her
he thought of Margaretta. He could sense her gloating
in the background.

Thinking about his wife filled him with remorse.
He could see the hurt in her eyes as the sister lorded
it over her. There came a knock upon the bedroom
door, gentle yet firm.

'Come in,' Jack called. It was the chambermaid
who had awakened him the morning before. Again
she carried a tray.

'What day have we?' Jack asked.

'It's Monday sir.'

'Great God almighty!' Jack exclaimed, 'and will
you tell me what time is it?'

'It's eight o'clock in the morning sir.'

Upon hearing this he groaned and buried his face in
his hands. He ran his fingers through his hair and
groaned again and again.

'Is something up sir?' the chambermaid's voice was

filled with alarm.

'I wish I was dead,' said Jack Murphy. For the first time he noticed the girl. She was young, no more than eighteen but she had a sympathetic face and sympathy was exactly what Jack needed just then. The source didn't worry him. While she poured his tea he launched into a full account of his adventures. She listened carefully and when he had finished she nodded her head sagely.

'I wouldn't worry too much,' she told him. 'You still have the money and that's a good start.'

'Oh sure,' he said with an edge of sarcasm, 'but 'tis me and not you that has to face them.'

'All you have to do,' she told him bluntly, 'is buy a fur coat for your wife. I promise you there won't be a word out of her if you land back with a good quality fur coat.'

'A fur coat,' he said and pondered her suggestion. 'But where would I get one?'

'Look,' she said kindly, 'I have an hour off at twelve. If you like I could meet you outside and show you where to go.'

'Good God,' said Jack gratefully, 'that would be great, great entirely.'

At twelve o'clock she was as good as her word. At ten past they were walking up Grafton Street. At half past they had narrowed the selection down to two.

One was a musquash at one hundred and fifty pounds and the other a Canadian squirrel at one hundred and forty. They decided upon the musquash.

'Listen,' said the salesman confidently. He spoke as if he were doing them a very considerable personal favour.

'Why not take both. You pay for them now. When

you arrive home let her decide for herself. You can return the one she doesn't want and we will only be happy to refund your money.'

This seemed to be an excellent idea.

'There is one other thing,' said Jack Murphy to the salesman, 'my wife is a very thrifty sort of woman so like a good man will you knock down the prices a bit.'

'We shall have no problem at all in that respect,' the salesman assured them. He produced two price tags, one marked thirty and the other twenty-five pounds. He attached the thirty pound tag to the musquash and the twenty-five to the Canadian squirrel. Jack returned with his parcels to the hotel where he bade goodbye to his young friend. He thrust a ten pound note into her hand as they parted.

It was late that night when he arrived home. It goes without saying that he was coolly received. His wife had no word of welcome for him, no word that is, until he produced the parcels. Proudly he ripped them open. He presented her with the musquash explaining that the other was on appro.

His wife was enchanted. She pressed the coat against her body and caressed it with her free hand.

That night Jack Murphy slept the sleep of the just. In the morning he received his breakfast in bed. His wife sat on the edge fondly watching him as he ate.

'I have good news for you,' she said.

'What would that be?' Jack asked absently.

'You needn't bother to return the other coat. Margaretta thinks it a steal at twenty-five pounds and she's decided to keep it.'

5

The Change

The village slept. It was always half asleep. Now,
because there was a flaming sun in the June sky, it
was really asleep. It consisted of one long street with
maybe forty to fifty houses on either side. There
were shops, far too many of them, and there were
three decaying public houses the doors of which
were closed as if they were ashamed to admit people.
No, that isn't quite true. The truth is that passing
strangers upset the tenor of normal life. The locals
only drank at night, always sparingly, and were therefore reluctant to accept habits that conflicted with
their own.

In the centre of the roadway a mangy Alsatian
bitch sunned herself inconsiderately and that was all
the life there was. The day was Friday. I remember it
well because my uncle with whom I was staying had
cycled down to the pier earlier that morning for two
fresh mackerel. Mackerel always taste better when
they are cooked fresh.

Anyhow, the bitch lay stretched in the sun. From
where I sat inside the window of my uncle's kitchen
I could see the street from one end to the other. At
nights when he didn't go to the pub that's what we
would do; sit and watch the neighbours from the
window. It was his place to comment and I would

listen, dodging away to my room sometimes to write
down something of exceptional merit. He was a great
commentator but I never complimented him. He
might stop if I did. It was hard, at times, to keep back
the laughter although on rare occasions I was unable
to smother it sufficiently and he would look at me
suspiciously.

Behind me I could hear him in the kitchen. He
made more noise than was strictly necessary.

'What way do you want it,' he called, 'boiled or
fried?'

'Fried. Naturally.'

At the far end of the village a smart green sportscar
came into view. Its occupants were a boy and a girl.
One minute the car was at the end of the street and
the next it was braking furiously to avoid collision
with the Alsatian bitch.

'What's happening out there?' But he didn't wait
for my reply.

He was standing beside me with the frying pan in
his hand. The car had stopped and the driver climbed
out to remove the obstacle.

'Come on. Come on. Get up outa that, you lazy
hound.'

Slowly the bitch turned over on her side and
scratched the ranges of twin tits which covered her
belly. She rose painfully and without looking at the
driver slunk to the pavement where she immediately
lay down again.

By this time a number of people stood in the doorways of their houses. The squeal of brakes had pene-
trated the entire village and they had come to invest-
gate. I followed my uncle to the doorway where we
both stood silently watching the girl. She had eased

herself from her seat and was now standing with hands on hips. She was tall and blonde. The tight-fitting red dress she wore clung to her body the way a label sticks to a bottle.

'Very nice. Very nice, indeed,' my uncle said.

'I think,' the girl told the driver, 'I'll take off this dress. I feel clammy.'

'Suit yourself,' he replied. With that he returned to his seat and lit a cigarette. The red dress was buttoned right down the front.

'What's the name of this place?' she asked as she ripped the topmost botton. From the way she said it we knew that she couldn't care less.

'Don't know,' the driver said. Then, as an after-thought, 'don't care.'

She shrugged her slender shoulders and set to work on the other buttons, oblivious to the wide eyes and partly open mouths of the villagers. A door banged a few houses away but it was the only protest. When she reached the bottom buttons she was forced to stoop but she didn't grunt the way the village women did. Another shrug and the dress flowed from her to the ground.

Underneath she wore chequered shorts and a red bra, no more. The driver didn't even look when she asked him to hand her the sweater which was under-neath her seat. Fumbling, his hand located the garment and he tossed it to her. He did make a comment however.

'Godsake hurry up,' he said with some irritation.

'Did you ever see such a heartless ruffian?' My uncle folded his arms and there was a dark look on his face. The girl stood for a moment or two shaking dust or motes or some such things from the sweater.

Her whole body rippled at every movement. She
started to pull the sweater over her head and then an
astonishing thing happened. Nobody was prepared for
it and this is probably why no one ever spoke about it
afterwards. Everybody thought about it afterwards.
I'm pretty certain of that.

Quite accidentally, I'm sure of that too, while she
was adjusting her neck and shoulders so that she
could the better accommodate the sweater, one of
her breasts popped out into the sunlight. There were
gasps. More doors banged.

A woman's voice called, 'Hussy. Hussy.'

Obviously she didn't hear. It was a deliciously pink
living think, dun-nippled and vital.

'Do 'em good,' my uncle whispered. 'Give 'em
something to think about.'

The sweater in place, the girl adjusted her close-
cropped hair. It didn't need adjusting but girls always
seem to adjust their hair when it least needs it.

She picked up the dress and with her fingers felt
the bonnet of the car. It must have been hot because
she took the fingers away quickly and covered the
bonnet with the dress. She then sat on the bonnet
and from nowhere produced a tube of lipstick. All
the while the driver sat looking straight in front of
him. He threw the cigarette away before it had
burned to the halfway stage. Now he sat with folded
arms and hooded eyes that saw nothing.

The girl, her lips glistening, neatly folded the dress,
went round to the boot of the car, flicked a button
and tucked in the dress. Closing the boot she looked
up and down the street. Her eyes scanned the few
remaining faces with interest. If she noticed any
reaction she did not show it in the least. For an instant

her eyes met those of my uncle. He winked almost imperceptibly but she must have noticed it because she permitted herself the faintest glimmer of a smile as she entered the car. She punched the driver playfully and to give him his due he caught her round the shoulders and planted a swift kiss on the side of her face. Gears growled throatily and the car leaped forward into sudden life. In an instant it was gone and I was old enough to know that it had gone forever.

Later when we had eaten our mackerel we went to drive in the cows for the evening milking. This was the part of the day I liked best. The morning and afternoon hours dragged slowly and lamely but as soon as the evening milking was done there was the prospect of some excitement. We could cycle down to the pier and watch the lobster boats arriving home or we could go to the pub and listen.

On that particular evening we decided on the pub. Earlier while we were eating he had said that things would never be the same again. 'At least,' he confided, 'not for a hell of a long time anyway.' I had pressed him for an explanation.

'Look,' he said, 'I don't know exactly how to put it but that girl we saw changed things.'

'In what way?' I asked.

'Oh, damn,' he said, not unkindly, 'you have me addled. How do I know in what way? Is this the thanks I get for cooking your mackerel?'

'Aren't you afraid I'll grow up in ignorance? He was fond of saying this when I failed to show interest in things he considered to be important. But he didn't rise to it. Instead he said: 'Wait and see. Wait and see, that's all.'

We went to the pub earlier than usual. He shaved

before we left the house which was unusual for him. Most men in the village shaved only on Saturday nights or on the eve of holy days.

The pub was cool. There was a long wooden seat just inside the door. We sat and he called for a pint of stout and a bottle of lemonade. There were two other customers. One was a farmer's boy I knew by sight and the other was the young assistant teacher in the local boys' school.

'There was a lot of hay knocked today,' the publican said when he had served the drinks and collected his money.

'There was indeed,' my uncle answered piously, 'and if this weather holds there will be a lot more knocked tomorrow.'

I gathered from this that he was at the top of his form. He was saying nothing out of the way. Nobody could possibly benefit from his words. He would go on all night like this relishing the utterly meaningless conversation.

The young teacher who was not a native of the place finished his drink and called for another. There was an unmistakable belligerence about him.

'A chip-carrier,' the uncle whispered, 'if ever I saw one.'

'What about the strip-tease act today,' the teacher ventured. When no one answered him he went to the window and looked out.

'Nothing ever happens here,' he pouted.

'True for you,' said the uncle.

He joined the teacher at the window. The three of us looked out into the street.

'Deserted,' the teacher said.

'Terrible,' from the uncle.

A couple came sauntering up the street.

'Here's up Flatface,' the teacher complained. Flat-face was the name given to Mrs O'Brien. She had the largest number of children in the village. She wasn't an attractive woman. Neither was her husband an attractive man. But tonight Mrs O'Brien looked different. She wore make-up and her hair was freshly washed and combed.

'That's a change,' my uncle said.

'He'll have her pregnant again,' the teacher protested.

Other couples appeared on the street, husbands and wives who were never seen out together. Some were linking arms. All the pairs walked ingratiatingly close to one another.

'What is this?' the teacher asked anxiously, 'what's happening?'

'Strange,' said the uncle.

Later when the pub closed we walked down the street together. On the doorway of the house next to ours a man and his wife were standing. She wore her Sundays and he leaned heavily on her shoulder.

'I know he's leaning on her,' said the uncle, 'but for him that's a lot.'

Two girls were sitting on the window ledge of the house at the other side.

'Come in for a cup of tea, Jack,' one said. My uncle hesitated.

'Ah, come on, Jack,' said the other, 'it's early yet.'

The young teacher stood at the other side of the street, legs crossed, back propped against the wall. He looked gangly, wretched and lost.

'Care for a drop of tea?' the uncle called across. Suddenly the teacher sprang into action. He checked first by looking up and down to confirm that it was really he who was being invited. Then fully assured he bounded across the roadway, a mad hunger for companionship in his eyes.

The uncle explained to the girls how he would have to see me safely indoors but promised he would be back in a matter of moments. He suggested that meanwhile they start the proceedings without him. Courteously, or rather gallantly, the teacher stood aside to allow the ladies first passage indoors. One giggled but covered her mouth in atonement when the other nudged her to stop. In our own house the uncle poured me a glass of milk and we sat at the table for a spell.

'See what I mean?' he said. 'I told you things would never be the same.'

I nodded that I fully understood.

'Was that why you shaved tonight?' I asked.

'No,' he answered, 'but I can see now it was a good job I did.'

6

The Fort Field

'Grass for ten cows and water for a million!' The old man laughed when he said it.

It was a long time ago. We were driving the cows down the bohareen for the evening milking. We were in a hurry. There was to be a football game that evening in Castleisland. A Tralee team was coming and there was talk of a needle. Through the yellow whins that stood out against the green hedges I could see his small fields, some still glinting sogginess in the height of summer.

'There's a play here,' I told myself. The old man is the hero and his wife is the heroine. The ten cows and the other livestock are the characters all but one. I am the chorus. You notice I leave the villian till last. Yet he was there from the very beginning. He is the water, the ever-present, the everlasting, the accursed water.

The old man used to boast good-humouredly in public houses that a man on horseback could not ride round the whole of his farm in a day. Strangers would shake their heads in incredulity but those who knew his terrain would wait patiently for the explanatory footnote.

' 'Tis true for me,' the old man would say. 'Horse and rider would be drowned after the Fort Field.'

As we neared the white-washed cow-stall, next to

the dwelling-house at the little road's end, we leaned over the five-bar gate to look into this field. It was a special place with a character of its own, snug as a carpeted parlour with a green more vivid than any of its neighbours. It was covered with good quality clover and natural vetches, the kind of field the man above makes especially to compensate for all the other squelchy, boggy acres. In spite of the fact that it was surrounded by inferior pastures it yet managed to remain aloof. It was similar in appearance to the excellent land one sees through a train window as one nears Dublin and I often asked myself what it was doing in the middle of total strangers.

It was so-called because of an ancient redan which occupied its furthest corner with its apex facing towards the gate. There were many such archaic redoubts in the district, but none had the purpose or individuality of this particular one.

The field comprised one acre, one rood and thirty-two perches. Needless to mention, it was pampered. It was conceded more cartloads of dung than any of the others and it was well-supported with annual investments of lime. Nothing was too good for it. It was the best-drained on the whole farm and I suspect it was a showpiece.

In spite of our hurry we lingered at the gate. I knew he would make no move until I spoke. I knew what was expected of me. I climbed onto one of the concrete piers and donned my admiration look.

'That's a powerful parcel of land,' I said after a little while. To this he made no reply, but from his even breathing I knew I had registered.

' 'Tis as fine a bit of land,' I went on, 'as you'd find if you footed it from Portmagee to Tarbert Island.'

He patted a passing cow on the rump but said nothing. This was to show how modest he was. He always pretended he didn't care.

'It's a field,' I said, 'fit for a racehorse.'

He spoke then, for the first time.

''Tisn't bad,' he admitted. ''Tisn't the worst anyhow.'

For a man who was supposed to be in a hurry he showed little inclination towards getting a move on. I knew I had better bring things to a close; otherwise we might miss the football game. I had to end on the highest possible note and so I racked my brain for a conclusive compliment. He was expecting it. He tapped one foot impatiently.

''Tis a land worth fighting for,' I said suddenly, remembering the phrase from a school book.

'That's good,' he said, repeating the words after me.

'A land worth fighting for. That's very good indeed.'

As we walked down the road he took a shilling from his pocket and handed it to me. The shilling was owing to me in the first place but I didn't think it would come so soon. After the cows were milked there was another surprise. This time it was for the cows. Instead of turning them into the inches by the small river I was instructed to allow them into the Fort Field.

They truly appreciated the gesture for when I opened the gate they thundered past me, bellowing delightedly with their tails cocked high.

In Castleisland when the football game was over we repaired to a public house. Country folk, in those days, would leave their custom with traders who hailed orignally from their own part of the world, so that when a farmer's son set up a business in a nearby town he could be sure of the support of the folk who came from his own townland and thereabouts.

Men who stand behind the bars of public houses have to be diplomatic or go broke. The publican we visited was no exception. At one time he had been a neighbour of the old man's. His greeting was warm and tactful and when he had dried his hands with a cloth he extended one to each of us in turn.

'How're the men?' was the first thing he said. This was clever because not only did it embrace us both but it gave me a dimension for which all boys long. I liked him immediately but when he winked at me and pulled upon his waxed moustache my heart went out to him altogether.

Our drinks were ordered, delivered almost at once, and paid for.

'Did you start cutting yet?' the publican asked.

'Indeed I did not,' the old man replied, 'but if this fine spell continues it could well be that I might be tempted.'

'There's a lot of hay down,' a listener put in.

'Meadows are light,' the old man countered. 'It's nothing but vanity.'

Talk ebbed and flowed. The bar began to fill and as time went by the speeches grew longer and a little louder. Men who were silent earlier could not be deterred from commenting on any and all subjects that came up for discussion.

All round us post-mortems on the game were in full swing.

'You'll never beat a Tralee team while the ball is dry,' a man with a pipe in his hand pointed out.

'That may be,' said another, 'but I tell you that Castleisland should have made more use of the wings.

When you play the wings you draw the backs and when you draw the backs you get the openings.'

When there was a lull in trade the publican returned to us. He leaned out over the high counter.

'How many cows are you milking presently?' he asked.

'Ten,' the old man answered.

'Any heifers?'

'Two.'

'Calves?'

'Four.'

It was plain to see that he had little relish for this sort of conversation. It was altogether too banal and unlikely to strike an interesting note.

'That's a nice field,' the publican tried a new tack, 'the one with the five-bar gate and the old fort in it.'

Immediately the old man sat bolt upright. The conversation had taken a turn to his liking. The publican, realising he had scored, pressed home his advantage.

'You could sleep on it,' he said, 'and you wouldn't know the difference from a mattress.'

We were quite taken by this. The old man called for another drink. He included two countrymen who sat on stools beside us.

When farmers meet over a drink it is not to discuss art or politics and when they argue it is never about religion unless a parish priest is building a new church and is expecting a fixed amount per head of cattle. Farmers talk about the slips and stores and well-bred boars and when they elaborate, which is rarely, they mostly unfold on the theme of drainage grants or certified seed potatoes. Overall the talk would be of wet land and dry and when the Fort Field was thrust into the conversation it was inevitable that it would hold the limelight for a goodly spell.

'There is no field like it in this neck of the woods,' the old man announced. The others nodded sagely and sipped their mediums of porter.

'And I don't mind tellin' you,' he went on, 'that a lot of folk I could mention has their eye on it.'

He submitted the latter part in undertone so that I wouldn't hear for I knew well that there was nobody interested in it but himself.

'I'm told,' said the publican, who had returned to us again, 'that if you searched it high and low in wintertime you wouldn't find an eggcup of water in it.'

'Nor as much as would fill a thimble,' the old man supported. This was followed by a long silence since nobody present could think of anything better to say and so pleasant was the atmosphere and so nicely turned the claims put forward that contradiction would have been sacrilegious.

The talk flowed on like a soft stream and subjects from the warble fly to artificial manure were touched upon. Then, out of the blue, the old man said to nobody in particular ' 'Tis a land worth fighting for.'

All within earshot cocked their ears at the profundity of this and the two men who had joined us repeated the phrase lovingly lest it be damaged in transit from one mouth to another. Others, out of earshot originally, fastened on it secondhand and uttered it over and over to themselves and to others. The statement puzzled some and a few, not in the know, dismissed it altogether because they could not appreciate the significance of it. By and large it was well received and the majority, although they might never admit it, stored it away for use at some appropriate time in the future.

Before we realised it the time for closing had come. The publican struck the tall counter three times with a wooden mallet.

'Time for the road boys,' he said. Without a word every man downed his drink and quietly we trooped out into the moonlight.

Later on, in bed, the sleep came quickly. It was good to stretch tired limbs on a soft feather tick I have forgotten what time it was the old woman came into my room. All I recall is waking up to find her hand shaking my shoulder.

'What's up?' I asked drowsily.

'It's that cracked man of mine,' she complained. 'He can't sleep and wants you out a minute.'

I rose and went into the next room. He sat propped by pillows on the bed. His pipe was in his mouth and billows of smoke issued from between his clenched teeth.

'It's gone from me,' he said.

'What's gone from you?' I asked.

'What you said this evening about the Fort Field.'

'Oh that,' I laughed.

'It's no laughing matter,' he said crossly. 'I'm awake half the bloody night over it.'

' 'Tis a land worth fighting for,' I reminded him. He smiled at once and grasped the words as if they were his long lost brothers.

'Ah yes,' he said serenely and he placed his pipe on the bedside table. He flattened the pillows, lay back on the bed and drew the quilt under his chin. A smile of supreme contentment transformed his face.

'A land worth fighting for,' he whispered half to himself. Then the snores came and he was deep in sleep.

7

'You're on Next Sunday'

You'll find more than a few to tell you that there isn't a word of truth in the following story and the nearer you come to the place where it happened you'll find a lot more. When I taxed the man who told me the story with these facts he took his pipe from his mouth, spat into the fire and looked me between the eyes for an embarrassingly long spell. He did not speak but when he returned the pipe to his mouth I knew that the tale was true and that those who belied it were either knaves or fools.

It happened on the fifteenth day of August in the year of our Lord, as they say in these parts, nineteen hundred and thirty-four. It was a fair year for primroses, a better one for hay and a woeful year for funerals.

The Fifteenth as it is still called locally is the annual Pattern Day in the lovely seaside resort of Ballybunion. From all quarters of Kerry, Cork and Limerick would come thousands of country people in every mode of conveyance from bike to omnibus to shanks' mare and pony cart. They still come but in nothing like the vast numbers of yore.

That particular Fifteenth, as I recall, broke fair and clear. Skies were blue. The air was fresh and wholesome and there was a hearty trace of fine breeze from the west. At the creameries and dispensaries that morning man, woman and child wore happy faces.

' 'Tis a great day for the Fifteenth,' they would say to each other and back would come the reply, 'ah sure 'tis a great day entirely.' At quarter to eleven in the noon of the day my grand-uncle Morrisheen Digley went forth to the haggard to catch the pony and at the turn of the noon he set forth for Ballybunion in his newly varnished trap. It would do your heart good to see the dancing legs of the pony and the squinting sparks on the flinty road when his iron-shod hooves made light of the long haul. I did not go on the occasion. He said I was too young. Instead he called for his old crony Thady Dowd of Lacca. Neither of the two was under seventy but none gamer set out that day for Ballybunion.

They untackled the pony in the back yard of Mikey Joe's American Bar and celebrated their arrival at the Pattern with two glasses of potstill whiskey. This was followed by a brace of pints, pints of creamy black porter. These were consumed so that the remains of the whiskey might be entirely scoured from the gullet, a most advisable practice this if one is to believe those who are fond of indulging in such procedural drinking.

Towards evening they walked as far as the beach to savour the salt sea air and to partake of a paddle near the shore. According to the old people there was nothing the equal of a paddle in the salt water to cure what might be wrong with you. It was pleasant on the shore. The fresh Atlantic breeze was sharp and bracing but as yet without its late autumnal sting. There were hundreds like themselves pacing up and down, ankle deep in the water, content to dawdle aimlessly until the anxiety for drink returned.

In the village they met neighbours from the townland of Lacca and between them they started a sing-
song in one of the public houses. When darkness fell a
great hunger for meat seized them. They repaired to a
café where they were served with succulent steaks
and roast potatoes. This was followed by two dishes
of rich trifle and the lot was washed down by several
cups of strong, well-sugared tea.

'This will make a handy base for more drink,' my
grand-uncle announced to Thady Dowd. Dowd nodded
agreement happily. So far the pair had enjoyed themselves thoroughly and the night was still but a starry-
eyed child in swaddling clothes. The best was to come.
After the meal they embarked on a grand tour of the
village pubs and they had a drink in every single one.

At this stage the reader will begin to raise an eye-
brow or two and wonder what is the purpose in the
retelling of such a commonplace narrative. Was not
their visit to the Pattern but a replica of other years,
a common jaunt indulged in by thousands of others
and all following the same predictable course?

Patience dear reader and bear with me. As soon as
the time came to close the pubs three pairs of well-
made civic guards appeared on the street and by their
presence ensured that every tavern was cleared. The
publicans were grateful enough for theirs had been a
long and arduous day. By this stage Thady Dowd and
my grand-uncle had more than their share of strong
drink but for the purpose of shortening the road
home they invested in a half pint of whiskey apiece at
Mikey Joe's American Bar.

Earlier they had plied the pony with a sufficiency
of oats and when they came to tackle him they found

him in excellent fettle. Like all animals who have spent a long day away from the green pastures of home he was full of taspy for the task before him. As soon as he found the open road free from obstacles he started to jogtrot in real earnest. Overhead a full moon lit up the countryside and the sky, it's full complement of stars visible in all it's quarters, shone like a treasure-house. In the body of the trap the semi-drunken companions sang at the top of their voices to the steady accompaniment of the pony's clopping hooves.

They sang song after song and from time to time they would uncork their whiskey bottles and partake of wholesome slugs. This made them sing all the louder and soon every dog in the countryside was responding. There was an unholy cacophany as the miles fell behind them.

Then, suddenly, for no reason whatsoever the pony stopped in his tracks and despite their most earnest entreaties would not be coaxed into moving a single, solitary inch.

'What's the matter with the creature anyway?' Thady Dowd asked indignantly.

'Beats me,' said my grand-uncle. All around there was an unearthly silence save for the chuckling of the Gale River which lay just ahead of them spanned by a narrow bridge. It was the same Gale that poor Spenser the poet did not forget when he wrote about Irish Rivers. On the left the crosses and tombstones of Gale Churchyard stood pale and grey in the drenching moonlight. The pony stood rooted to the roadway, head bent, his whole frame taut and tense. There was white foam at the corners of his mouth and a look of abject terror, terrible to behold, in his bloodshot eyes.

'I don't like the look of things,' my grand-uncle whispered.

'A rattling damn I don't give,' Dowd shouted, 'I'm getting out of here to see what the matter is.'

'Stay as you are,' my grand-uncle counselled but there was no stopping the headstrong Dowd. He jumped on to the roadway and walked round trap and pony several times.

'There's nothing here,' he called out. He then proceeded towards the river thinking that some calamity might have overtaken the bridge and that the pony, with its animal instinct, might have sensed this. The bridge was in perfect order. Dowd looked over its twin parapets into the shallow, warbling water. He could see nothing unusual.

He retraced his steps and with a scornful toss of his grey head went towards the graveyard of Gale. As soon as he entered the little by-road which led to the gateway the pony lifted its head and followed slowly. It is well to remember that at no time did my grand-uncle leave the trap. He sat stiffly, holding the reins, carefully following his friend's every move.

When Dowd leaned across the gate of the graveyard he emitted a loud yell of genuine surprise. There before him were two hurling teams dressed in togs, jerseys and slippers. Every hurler had a hurley in his hand and at one side sitting on a low tombstone sat a small inoffensive-looking, bald-headed man. He wore a white jersey as distinct from the two teams who wore red and green respectively. He had a sliotar or hurley ball in one hand and in the other he held an ancient, burnished, copper hunting horn.

The pony had stopped dead a second time opposite the gateway over which Dowd was leaning.

'Come away out of that,' my grand-uncle called out, 'and leave the dead to themselves.'

'What's the use?' Dowd called back, 'the pony won't budge till it suits these people.'

'What's the matter?' he called out to the hurlers who stood about as if they were waiting for something special to happen. At first no one heeded him but when he called out belligerently a second time a tall player with a face the colour of limestone approached the gate. He explained to Dowd that he was the captain of the red-jerseyed hurlers but that the game could not start because his team was short a man.

'Who are these teams anyway?' Dowd asked cheekily. The captain explained that his team was Ballyduff and the other team Ballybawn.

'Ho-ho,' cried Dowd exultantly. 'I'm your man. My mother, God be good to her, was a Ballyduff woman. If you have no objection I will play with your team.'

The captain nodded silently and when my grand-uncle called to Dowd to abandon his arrant foolishness the captain turned and addressed him where he sat in the trap.

'Not an inch will you or your pony move,' said he in a hollow, haunted voice, 'until the final horn is sounded in this game of hurling.' My grand-uncle said no more. The pony stood now like a statue and the sounds of the river were no longer to be heard. Overhead the moon shone brightly and the pitch which was the length and breadth of the graveyard, was illuminated as though it were floodlit. Forms appeared from the ground and sat themselves on the graveyard wall. The referee looked upwards at the moon and after a few moments wait blew upon the hunting horn. Then he threw in the ball.

The exchanges started slowly enough with Dowd's team, Ballyduff, getting the worst of it from a faster Ballybawn side. The first score came when the referee awarded a free puck to Ballybawn. He also cautioned a number of the Ballyduff players, notably Dowd and the captain, for abusive language towards himself and for dirty play in general.

The Ballybawn skipper drove the ball straight between the uprights. On the graveyard walls the partisans went wild and a fist fight broke out near the gate. Somebody flung an empty cocoa cannister at the refereee and he threatened to call off the game if the crowd did not behave themselves. There were a number of fistic exchanges on the field of play but by and large the standard of hurling was as good as my grand-uncle had seen for many a day. There were many fluent movements and excellent long-range scores. The wrist work and pulling left little to be desired. Half time came and went and now the two teams were playing for all they were worth. Time was slipping away and with five minutes to go the sides were level.

Neither would yield an inch. Every player strove manfully to register the single score that would put his own team ahead of the other. The ghostly forms jumped up and down on the walls egging the players on to greater deeds.

It seemed as if the game must end in a draw and the grand-uncle noted that from time to time the referee looked nervously at the full moon and feverishly fingered his hunting horn, anxious for full time to roll round so that he might wash his hands of the whole affair. There is nothing a referee loves so dearly as a drawn game. The hopes of both sides are kept alive and it is unlikely that he will be assaulted as he leaves the pitch. With less than a minute remaining there was a mêlée at midfield in which Dowd was involved. Fists flew and hurleys were raised. More than once could be heard the clash of ash against doughty skulls.

The referee intervened and taking a scroll from his togs' pocket he commenced the business of taking names. It was during this lull that Dowd sat on a convenient tombstone to savour a richly-merited breather. He withdrew the half pint bottle from his trousers pocket and dolefully surveyed the remnants of his whiskey. The bottle was still quarter full. He raised it to his lips and without once taking it from his head swallowed the contents. Almost immediately he heaved a great sigh which could be heard all over the graveyard. Then he tightened his trousers' belt and waited for play to resume.

With seconds remaining the hunting horn was sounded yet again and the ball was thrown in. Dowd it was who won possession. With a fierce and drunken yell he cut through his opponents like a scythe through switch-grass with the ball poised on the base of his hurley. There were times when he darted like a trout and times when he bounded like a stag. He leaped over gravemounds and skirted crosses and tombstones at breakneck speed. All the time he edged his way nearer the opposing goal line.

Seeing an opening on the left wing he seized his chance and headed straight for the goal with the entire Ballybawn team on his heels like a pack of hungry hounds. Thirty yards out he stopped dead and took a shot. The ball went away to the right but if it did it

passed through the eye of a Celtic cross and rebound-
ed off the head of a plaster angel. The rebound was
deflected towards the goal by the extended hand of
the figure of Michael the Archangel. It skeeved* the
left upright and found its way to the back of the net.
Need I mention that while the ball was travelling so
was the empty whiskey bottle which Dowd, with
sound foresight, had flung at the Ballybawn goal-
keeper as soon as the referee's back was turned. The
crowd went wild. The Ballyduff team and supporters
milled around Dowd and embraced him. Then they
lifted him aloft and trotted round the graveyard on a
lap of victory. Finishing the lap the Ballyduff captain
called for three cheers for their visitor. Three eerie
ullagones went heavenwards and died slowly till the
muted river sounds took over once more. The teams
had suddenly vanished save for the tall, ghostly presence of the Ballyduff captain. For the first time in
over an hour the pony stirred. He pawed the dirt
roadway, anxious for the high road.

'Come on at once,' my grand-uncle called. Dowd,
escorted by the captain, made his way towards the
gate where the pony was now prancing and difficult
to restrain. Dowd shook hands with the captain and
was about to depart when a ghostly hand was laid
firmly on his right shoulder. The captain leaned forward and whispered into Dowd's ear. Whatever it was
he said Dowd's face underwent a terrible change. The
glowing red nose was now puce-coloured and the rosy,
whiskey-tinted cheeks were ashen grey. Slowly,
almost painfully, he climbed across the gate while the
captain faded like a breeze-driven mist behind him.

* Skimmed.

In the trap Dowd was silent and thoughtful. On his face was a woebegone look that struck a chill in my grand-uncle's heart. The pony highstepped his way homewards, his dark mane flowing loosely behind him, his firm rump bobbing up and down as the miles passed by.

Finally my grand-uncle popped the question.

'What in heaven's name did he say to you?' he asked. Dowd shook his head sadly before he replied. Then he spoke slowly and deliberately with a crack in his voice.

'He informed me,' Dowd announced, 'that because of the way I played tonight I would be on for good next Sunday.'

8

Jonathan

The rhododendrons were in full bloom. White and
scarlet and puce, profuse and gay they brightened the
long avenue that led to the old house. He could not
see it yet but any moment now it would present itself.
Surely it would be round the next bend. It seemed as
if he had been walking for miles and miles, for hours
and hours. It wasn't the tiredness that bothered him.
It was the boredom. He had not met a single creature
since entering the avenue a half hour before. He had
spent most of the time dawdling, feeling the texture
of the rhododendrum petals or descending the grassy
slope to plop pebbles into the stream which accompanied the avenue from the beginning.

Jonathan was eleven. He was small for his age but
well-knit with good bones. From time to time he
would change the letter from one hand to the other.
That was the whole purpose of his journey, the letter.
He knew its contents by heart, not because he had
opened it but because he was partly responsible for
its composition.

He had helped Paddy Pine to write it. Paddy
worked with Jonathan's father on the farm and lived
in the farmhouse where he had a room of his own
overlooking the river. He was an orphanage boy
although he was now more of a man having passed

the twenty mark some months previously. He was fifteen when he first came to work with the Hindleys. Paddy Pine was a runaway. With another boy he scaled the orphanage wall one night and ran off to join the British army. That was in nineteen forty-one. An astonished Russia had just been invaded by a rampant Germany and the British recruiting offices were none too inquisitorial when a likely prospect proffered himself for enlistment. It was Paddy's intention to walk the two hundred miles from Kerry to the border town of Castleblayney. From there to the recruiting office in Newry on the other side of the border would be a mere formality. On their second day out they ran short of food and without letting him know, Paddy's friend returned to the orphanage. This did not deter him. He resolved to go on. On the morning of the third day Hilary Hindley, Jonathan's mother, found him in one of the outhouses. He was in high fever. It was almost a week before he was able to stand by himself. The kindness shown him by the Hindleys was something he could not fully comprehend. They had never seen him before. They owed him nothing yet while he was ill they tended to his every want. The children, young Jonathan and the twins Rose and Sheila who were a year older, spent all of their free time reading to him during his convalescence. As the days went happily by he began to feel guilty and fearful. There would be a hot reception awaiting him at the orphanage. He resolved to make a second break for the border at the first opportunity. He felt an unbearable pang of loneliness at the prospect of leaving the Hindleys. It was a thought he dared not dwell upon.

On the night before his planned departure Ned

Hindley took him aside.

'I should have reported finding you to the civic guards Paddy,' Ned started, 'but I couldn't find it in my heart to do it just then. I've kept putting it off and off but now the time has come when I have to.'

Paddy Pine said nothing. He nodded his head in resignation while Ned Hindley continued.

'If you still want to hit for the border the door is open to you and I'll see to it you get a good start with enough food and a pound or two in your pocket.'

'I want to stay here. I'll be your workman. I'll do anything,' Paddy cried out the words in anguish. Hilary Hindley came running from the kitchen.

'What did you do to him?' she said accusingly. She hurried towards Paddy and placed her arms round him protectively.

'I did nothing,' Ned Hindley said with a pained face. 'I just told him the score and he said he wanted to stay here. That's all.'

'If that's what he wants then that's the way it's going to be,' Hilary announced firmly.

'That might not be possible,' her husband warned.

'Well,' she said, 'you'd better make it possible or you'll be sleeping alone for a while.'

Ned Hindley knew his wife well enough to know that she meant what she said. Only once before did she issue such an ultimatum and when he failed to take her seriously he was left out in the cold for an unbearably long time.

'I'll do what I can,' he promised. There had been difficulties but the Hindleys were held in high regard locally and after a short, concessive period in the orphanage Paddy Pine was duly released into their hands. He had two qualities which endeared him to

Ned and Hilary from the beginning. The boy was refreshingly innocent and absolutely loyal. On the debit side he was not the brightest boy in the world and before he could grasp even the most elementary chore the directions had to be hammered home repeatedly. This apart, he was an able and willing farmhand and was completely happy at his work. As he grew older his shyness became more pronounced. He found it difficult to communicate with girls and despite every help from Ned and Hilary he made little headway in this field.

'Don't worry,' Ned said to his wife, 'when the right one comes along there'll be no holding him.'

'Yes,' she said seriously, 'but will he recognise the right one when he sees her?'

Time passed and Jenny Stevens entered Paddy Pine's life. It was to be some time before Jenny was to know about it. Paddy noticed her first at Mass. On a number of occasions she smiled at him but she would have no way of knowing his true feelings. She was the youngest of a large local family and as soon as she reached school-leaving age she was pressed into domestic service with a neighbouring farmer. The work was hard and the hours long. After a year she tired of it and found employment with the Misses Carter, Julie and Emily, who lived in the old house in what was left of the Carter demesne. Here the work was much lighter and hours shorter. Here too she was not discouraged when she used make-up or affected what the local people interpreted as airs and graces.

It was to the Carter house Jonathan was presently bound with the letter from Paddy Pine to Jenny Stevens. The contents of the letter were simple enough, an appeal without embellishments asking her to attend the Sunday night dance in the Parochial hall.

It was a task to Jonathan's liking. He revelled in any sort of intrigue and this, in his estimation, was intrigue of a high order. Suddenly the old house thrust itself into view. Three-stories, ivy-covered and Georgian, it stood elegantly and correctly at the end of the avenue. Built in 1820 by the great-grandfather of the present owners its regency façade at once impressed the visitor. Giant, ancient oaks and chestnuts stood aloofly and discreetly at either side dwarfing the rhododendrons which spread out to left and right around a gravelled frontage. In terms of character and distinction it easily outdid all the other residences in the parish.

The demesne consisted of two hundred acres. One hundred and fifty of these were of the finest pastureland. The other fifty were mostly woodland and scrub. It was the biggest holding for miles. In various local histories it was rather unflatteringly referred to as a typical Ascendancy dwelling-house. Whatever one may think of this the land was certainly Ascendancy-type in that it was the most fertile in the district.

'Fair play to the English,' Jonathan had once heard his father say, 'they never stole anything but the best.'

There was no ill-feeling in the way he said it. It was purely good-natured resignation. Jonathan stood for awhile where the avenue expanded and ended in the gravel frontage. He imagined all sorts of things. Who dared guess what baleful eyes might be peering at him from one of the large windows or what fiendish goings-on were carefully concealed behind the huge oaken door. In the nearby rhododendrons there was a faint stirring followed by an awesome silence. He bent

noiselessly and selected a polished rounded stone.
Taking careful aim he lobbed it into the exact spot in
the bushes where the sound had come from. Suddenly, explosively, a pair of protesting blackbirds erupted
from the depths, chattering insanely till they found
sanctuary further down the avenue. The noise
attracted a figure from the rear of the house. It was
Miss Emily, the younger of the Carter sisters. Emily
Carter was in her early seventies. In one hand she
carried a book and in the other an ancient walking
stick which she threateningly held aloft.

When she saw who it was she lowered the stick. 'I
thought it might be a stray dog,' she explained, 'they
come all the time to chase the cattle.'

'Who is it Emily?' her sister's voice called from the
side of the house.

'It's only Hilary Hindley's Jonathan,' Emily called
back.

'What does he want?' Miss Julie asked as soon as
she saw Jonathan.

'What is it you want?' Emily asked.

'I have a message for Jenny Stevens,' Jonathan
replied. Upon hearing this both women exchanged
knowing glances.

'I hope we have not come on a mission of maid-
filching,' Miss Julie said crossly. It was some time
before Jonathan was able to comprehend this.

'My mother never has a maid,' he answered after a
while in what he hoped was an equally cross tone.

'There's always a first time,' Miss Julie shot back.

'I have a letter from Paddy Pine for Miss Stevens,'
Jonathan blurted out, 'as soon as I give it to her I'll
be on my way.'

'She's beyond in the kitchen-garden picking gooseberries,' Emily informed him. 'When you give her the letter you can have strawberries and cream if you want some.'

'Thank you,' Jonathan inclined his head civilly in acknowledgement of the gesture.

'We're under the big cedar,' Miss Julie indicated a giant evergreen a little way from the house. 'We'll have a nice chat,' Miss Emily added. Jonathan took this to mean that the chat was to be the price of the strawberries. Chat was not the word he would apply to the string of questions the sisters would have stored up since his last visit. The odd thing was that he rarely answered truthfully and despite the fact that they knew this they were still willing to pose the questions. Jonathan guessed that they were entertained in some small way by what he told them and that possibly they were able to sift a few grains of truth from the great number of whoppers with which he presented them. He had no compunction about lying. Most of the questions were so outrageous that they deserved no better. Sometimes he suspected that they were testing the limits of his imaginative powers. With him it was a game. He was of the belief that it was the same with the sisters.

At first he could see no trace of Jenny Stevens in the ancient, walled kitchen-garden. It was a grossly overgrown place with every plant in dire need of pruning. The place was jittery with songbirds. They started from every bush and tree as he followed the old stone path to the glass-house.

It was here he encountered Jenny Stevens. She was not alone. Jonathan recognised Bill Lunty. Lunty was the farm manager. He was a dark-haired, lusty fellow with stunningly white teeth which he revealed by

means of a wide, ingratiating smile at every possible
opportunity. He had his arms around Jenny Stevens
who was making half-hearted attempts to resist him.
He kissed her fiercely but she succeeded in pushing
his head away. It was a type of kiss that Jonathan had
not seen before. It was certainly not the kind of kiss
he had so often seen his father give his mother, the
sort of kiss everybody in the household might join in.

'You stop at once,' Jenny was saying but beyond
this she did not remonstrate further. Jonathan was
surprised. She could have easily broken away if she
had wanted to. Bill Lunty kissed her again, this time
fully on the lips and afterwards on the face and neck.
He drew her firmly against him. She offered no resistance whatsoever. Jonathan spoke from the shade of
a dropping apple tree.

'Excuse me,' he said. Bill Lunty released the girl at
once. When Jenny saw who it was she slapped the
manager's face.

'You have a cheek,' she said with feigned anger.
Lunty advanced on Jonathan and lifted him by both
ears till their faces were level.

'What do you think you're doing?' he demanded
angrily.

'Nothing,' Jonathan replied as best he could from
his position above the ground. His ears were beginning
to hurt.

'Put him down at once,' Jenny called.

'Why should I?' Lunty retorted savagely.

'Because,' Jenny spoke with a trace of mockery,
'his father happens to be Ned Hindley.' It had the
desired effect. Jonathan was released.

'What do you mean?' Lunty shouted, 'sneaking up
on people without warning. Suppose I were to tell

your father?' Jonathan, thankful to be on the ground, decided against answering lest he inadvertently say something which might further provoke Lunty.

'Did you come to see me about something Jonathan?' Jenny asked politely. Jonathan tendered the letter. Jenny ripped it open at once and avidly read the solitary, crumpled sheet. Jonathan silently mouthed the message word for word in concert with her. He waited eagerly for her reaction.

'Tell that orphanage boy not to dare write to me again,' she spoke shrilly. It was a glorious opportunity for comparing her legitimate background with one which seemed, in her eyes, to be less favourable. She looked the very personification of righteous indignation, her extraordinarily pretty face flushed disdainfully, her stance proud and haughty.

'Let's have a look,' Lunty snatched the sheet from her hand and read it out loud. If his aim was to impress Jenny Stevens he was successful. She burst out laughing as he perfectly mimicked the reticent Paddy Pine.

'Could I have the letter back please?' Jonathan asked meekly.

'It's mine,' Jenny replied perkily. 'I'll keep it as a curio.' Jonathan said nothing. Slowly he turned and picked his way along the path. He ran quickly past the house to the amazement of the Misses Carter who awaited him under the big cedar.

'What do you suppose?' Miss Emily asked. There was no mistaking the disappointment in her voice.

'Boys,' Miss Julie replied, 'just boys. You can never tell with boys.'

Paddy Pine listened for the third time to Jonathan's account of his visit to the Carters. Jonathan had not told of seeing the kissing session. Things were bad enough without including that. Neither did he reveal that Lunty had read the letter.

'You're sure that was her excuse?' Paddy pressed him. 'That was exactly what she said,' Jonathan lied, 'tell him he's too young.'

'Nothing more? Nothing more?' In time the whole household came to know of the letter. For Jenny Stevens it was something of a romantic triumph. She showed it to less fortunate serving girls of her acquaintance. Word spread. It was an embarrassing period for Paddy Pine. He solved his problem by not going out at night. A month passed and the affair was forgotten.

Paddy's obsession with Jenny persisted. Neither Ned nor Hilary Hindley took it too seriously.

'We all must go through these phases,' Ned submitted.

'It's not calf love,' Hilary reminded him. 'It's something more. It's rather sad for Paddy that it's so onesided. Personally I don't like the girl.'

'You'll have to admit she's very pretty.'

'I agree on that score but I do not see her as an ideal partner for Paddy.'

'All she has to do is lift her little finger. He'll follow.'

'That's what worries me,' Hilary Hindley mused.

On his way from school Jonathan called each afternoon to the village post office where he would collect the newspaper. If he had pocket money he would indulge in an ice cream or a bar of chocolate. Generally he would spend a quarter hour browsing through comics and magazines. The assistant was a red-haired girl named Nora Devane. Jonathan thought highly of her, so highly he kept her at the back of his mind as a prospective girlfriend for Paddy. She never objected when he thoroughly read a new comic which he might not be able to afford. She was only seventeen. He found her easy and pleasant to converse with. In addition she had bright blue eyes and a pleasant smile.

Not long after his visit to the old house he resolved to have a word with Nora. Instinctively he knew that she would be a different proposition to Jenny Stevens. At least she would take him seriously. Of this he was convinced.

About a fortnight before Christmas while he was rummaging through the comic stand he succeeded in catching her eye. She came outside the counter as soon as she could.

'What is it Jonathan?' she asked.

'Will you go with Paddy Pine?'

'Why doesn't he come and ask me himself?'

'Because he's shy,' Jonathan told her.

'He's a nice boy,' she said half to herself. Then to Jonathan, 'I'll have to see. I just can't make up my mind all at once and anyway my mother likes me to tell her about dates. I'll let you know tomorrow.'

Faithfully after school Jonathan called at the post office.

'The answer is yes,' Nora whispered when she found it convenient to do so, 'but he'll have to ask me himself.'

That night before they fell asleep Jonathan paid a visit to Paddy's room. He sat on a small stool near the window and looked out into the river.

'It's high tonight,' he said. Paddy lay on his bed fully awake, looking at the ceiling.

'You didn't see her lately?' he asked.

'Only in the distance,' Jonathan answered.

'How can she be so cruel?' Paddy suddenly leaped from the bed and joined Jonathan at the window.

'All night I listen to the river and think of her,' he said. 'I think of little else. I try to drive her from my thoughts and think of other things but her face comes back from nowhere and I see her smile and laugh. I dream of her too. She runs along the river bank by the sallies and I follow.'

'I met somebody today who was asking for you,' Jonathan lied.

'Oh?' was all Paddy said.

'Yes,' Jonathan seized his opportunity, 'she'd like to go with you sometime.'

'Who are you speaking about?'

'You know Nora Devane, the girl with the red hair who works in the post office.'

'I know her. Why wouldn't I? Don't I see her every Sunday when we call for the papers.'

'She's a nice girl,' Jonathan said, 'I mean a really nice girl.'

'I'm sure she is,' Paddy sighed. He returned to the bed and drew the clothes over his head. Jonathan sat by the window watching the moonlight play where the water was broken. Suddenly he felt lonely. The moon submitted herself to the shrouding clouds and a giant shadow came down the river. He rose from the chair and addressed himself to the form in the bed.

'Will you consider her?' he asked hopefully.

Paddy Pine's head emerged from beneath the bed-clothes.

'Consider who?' he asked absently. Jonathan knew that further conversation would be a waste of time. For the next few days he entrusted the collection of

the newspaper to the twins. He decided he could not
very well face Nora Devane under the circumstances.
However, as Christmas drew near he was forced to
confront her. There were cards to be posted and gifts
to be bought.

'He never called,' was the first thing Nora said
when he entered the shop.

'I told you he was shy,' Jonathan returned.

'Well,' she pouted, 'if he's going to be that shy
where's the point?'

'Don't worry,' Jonathan assured her, 'he'll come
round to it.'

'Saint Stephen's night is only a week away,' she
reminded him.

Jonathan was well aware that the Saint Stephen's
night dance was the most important one of the year.
It was the accepted time for introducing new faces.
There was also the fact that the youth of the district
looked forward to it with an eagerness they did not
reserve for other occasions. This might well be due
to their being cooped up over the Christmas or it
could be that it was the finale of the year's festivities.
New Year's eve was less than a week later. Whatever it
was, nothing less than a calamity could keep the
young people home on that night.

'Do you think its likely he'll be in to see me before
Christmas?' Nora asked as soon as the shop was
empty of customers.

'Most likely,' Jonathan said.

'But how can I be sure?'

'You can be sure,' Jonathan said it emphatically
while he prayed that a customer would cross the
threshold and spare him from further interrogation.

'I'll have to be going now,' he told her, 'I'm late as

it is.'

'Jonathan Hindley,' she called after him, 'are you sure you're not having me on?'

Jonathan ran quickly down the little street and turned into a laneway pretending he hadn't heard. He dawdled on the way home. Sooner or later he would have to take the bull by the horns and tell the truth to Nora. It might not be too bad if he didn't like her, but the fact remained that she was the only person in the village who consistently showed him kindness.

At the entrance to the Carter demesne which he passed each afternoon on his way home he stopped to kick the carpeting of decaying leaves into a central mound.

So industrious was his assault that he failed to notice the figure in the rhododendrons immediately at his back. It was growing dusk at the time.

'Psst,' came the whispered summons from the mouth of the figure in question but this he dismissed as the utterance of some insect or animal in the undergrowth.

'Hey! You!' a girl's voice called impatiently. Jonathan was taken completely by surprise. He turned quickly as a girl with a headscarf tightly bound round her head appeared from the deepening dusk. Jonathan failed to identify her at first.

'Who... who's there?' he asked nervously. Cautiously he retreated a step. There had been talk some years previously of an apparition at this very entrance.

'Don't run away please,' the girl said. 'It's me, Jenny Stevens.'

'What is it you want?' Jonathan was still nervous.

'I've been waiting for you,' she said. 'I have to speak to you.'

'About what?'

'The Pine boy. Is he still interested do you think?'

'Yes,' Jonathan replied.

'You're sure?'

'Yes,' he told her, 'I'm sure.'

'I want you to give him a message. It's especially for him. Nobody else must know.' Jonathan nodded. He took advantage of her nearness to examine her face. She was very pretty but there were dark lines under her eyes and her cheeks were indrawn. All in all there was a gauntness about her face which gave it a frightened look.

'Nobody knows I'm here,' she said desperately. 'I've been waiting for nearly an hour. Are you always as late as this?'

Jonathan shook his head. There was an unexpected breathlessness about her that he associated with older women.

'Are you sick?' he asked.

'No. No,' she replied at once. 'I never felt better in my life. It's the cold. I've been standing here so long that it's got inside me. Why do you look at me like that?'

'I'm sorry,' he said awkwardly, 'you've changed somehow.'

'Am I less pretty?' she asked the question confidently.

'It's not that,' he said with difficulty.

'I know. I know,' she said quickly. 'I've lost weight. That's what it is. Now listen carefully Jonathan. You tell Paddy Pine that I'm leaving for England in the morning. Tell him to meet me here. The half eight bus stops right at this gate week mornings. I'll be waiting. You'll tell him that?'

'Yes,' Jonathan said. She gave him the message over and over and asked him to say it for her. He had to repeat himself again and again until she was assured that he had it correctly by heart.

'No matter what,' she insisted, 'nobody must know. I wouldn't like if anybody did and you know he wouldn't like it. Give me your oath that you'll tell nobody but him.'

'I can't give my oath,' Jonathan sounded adamant about it. 'That's a mortal sin.'

'Your word of honour then?'

'Alright,' he said. 'I give my word of honour.'

'You're a good boy,' she told him. 'Now hurry home and tell him. There will be things he must do.' Squeezing his arm she hurried up the avenue. He stood for a while deep in thought after she had gone. Slowly he made the sign of the cross and looked upwards.

'God,' he said, 'you heard me whisper that I was crossing out the promise of my word the moment I gave it. This is to make sure you heard.'

Darkness had fallen by the time he entered the brightly-lit kitchen of his home.

'What in God's name kept you Jonathan,' Hilary Hindley asked. 'Have you been fighting again?'

Jonathan shook his head. Hilary shook hers.

'Call your father and Paddy like a good boy. Supper's ready.'

After supper the rain fell. It drummed on the corrugated roofs of the outhouses. Everywhere rivulets were forming and running with increasing volume to the river. It was a steady, heavy rain that lasted well into the morning. Jonathan was out of bed by eight o'clock. At half past he hid himself close

by a stand of roadside spruce about fifty yards from
the Carter gate. There was no sign of the girl. He
waited patiently until he heard the faint rumble of
the approaching bus. As it neared the gate the gears
changed hoarsely and the outsize vehicle drew to a
squealing halt.

Suddenly Jenny Stevens appeared. Her head was
covered with a headscarf as before and she carried a
large suitcase in her hand. Her long, blue gaberdine
coat hung unbuttoned by her sides. Vainly she looked
up and down the road. Desperately she signalled to
the driver for a moment or two of grace. He waited a
full minute. Then he blew on the hooter. With a dark
look on her face she boarded the bus.

Paddy Pine lay on the bed. He had spent a melan-
choly day. At the creamery he learned of Jenny's
departure the day before. Everybody seemed to know
she had left for England. No particular person had
informed him. He had overheard.

Quietly Jonathan entered the room. He sat on the
stool by the window and looked out.

'The water's falling,' he said. 'I can tell by the
sound.' When Paddy failed to comment Jonathan
tried a new tack.

'Several have asked Nora Devane to the dance on
Saint Stephen's night. She doesn't know what to do.
What will I say to her?'

Paddy sat up on the bed.

'I don't know,' he said.

'I think you should come and ask her tomorrow
before it's too late.'

'But I hardly know her.'

'I think it's a terrible thing,' Jonathan announced
righteously, 'that a girl as good-looking as Nora Devane

should be left hanging there just because you won't ask her. It's you she wants. She said so. She must have told me ten times. She really likes you.'

'But how can she like me so much when I only know her to see her?'

'I don't know,' Jonathan replied. 'Just imagine that she likes you as much as you liked Jenny Stevens and you'll know what it's like for her.'

A thoughtful look settled on Paddy's face. He sat on the side of the bed. Jonathan guessed that he was puzzling out the implications of what he had just said. After a while Paddy spoke.

'I know what you mean,' he said.

'I'll see you in the village then, tomorrow after school. She'll be delighted.'

'You really think so?' There was a look of uncertainty on Paddy's face.

'I know so,' Jonathan concluded as he left the room hurriedly in case Paddy started to have misgivings.

Downstairs Ned and Hilary Hindley sat by the fire. Each was preoccupied, Ned with the day's paper and Hilary with a pullover which was to be part of Jonathan's Christmas box. Out of the blue Hilary spoke.

'I'm worried about Jonathan,' she said. Ned Hindley put the paper to one side.

'What's he been up to?' he asked.

'I don't know,' she said. 'He was two hours coming from school today and most of the time he acts as though his mind was elsewhere. You think he's a bright boy?' Ned Hindley laughed.

'I wouldn't worry about Master Jonathan,' he said. 'There's more to him than meets the eye.' Reassured Hilary resumed her knitting.

'Jenny Stevens is gone to England since yesterday,' Ned informed her.

'I'm not surprised,' Hilary sighed.

'She looked a bit peakish lately. You think there's something wrong?'

'I'm certain of it,' Hilary answered, 'and from the looks of her its been wrong with a while.'

MORE BOOKS by JOHN B. KEANE

LETTERS OF A SUCCESSFUL T.D.

This bestseller takes a humourous peep at the
correspondence of an Irish parliamentary deputy. Keane's
eyes have fastened on the human weaknesses of a man
who secured power through the ballot box, and
uses it to ensure the comfort of his family and friends.

LETTERS OF AN IRISH PARISH PRIEST

There is a riot of laughter in every page and its theme
is the correspondence between a country parish priest and
his nephew who is studying to be a priest. Fr O'Mora has
been referred to by one of his parishioner's as one who 'is
suffering from an overdose of racial memory aggravated
by religious bigotry'. John B. Keane's humour is neatly
pointed, racy of the soil and never forced. This book gives
a picture of a way of life which though in great part is
vanishing is still familiar to many of our countrymen who
still believe 'that priests could turn them into goats'. It
brings out all the humour and pathos of Irish life. It is
hilariously funny and will entertain and amuse everyone.

LETTERS OF AN IRISH PUBLICAN

In this book we get a complete picture of life in Knockanee as seen through the eyes of a publican, Martin MacMeer. He relates his story to his friend Dan Stack who is a journalist. He records in a frank and factual way events like the cattle fair where the people 'came in from the hinterland with caps and ash-plants and long coats,' and the cattle stood 'outside the doors of the houses in the public streets'. Through his remarkable perception we 'get a tooth' for all the different characters whom he portrays with sympathy, understanding and wit. We are overwhelmed by the charms of the place where at times 'trivial incidents assume new proportions.' These incidents are exciting, gripping, hilarious, touching and uncomfortable.

THE GENTLE ART OF MATCHMAKING and other important things

This book offers a feast of Keane, one of Ireland's best loved playwrights. The title essay reminds us that while some marriages are proverbially made in Heaven, others have been made in the back parlour of a celebrated pub in Listowel and none the worse for that! But John B. Keane has other interests besides matchmaking, and these pieces mirror many moods and attitudes. Who could ignore Keane on Potato-Cakes? Keane on skinless sausages? or Half-Doors? Is there a husband alive who will not recognise someone near and dear to him when he reads, with a mixture of affection and horror, the essay 'Female Painters'? And, more seriously, there are other pieces that reflect this writer's deep love of tradition: his nostalgic re-creation of an Irish way of life that is gone forever.

LETTERS OF A LOVE-HUNGRY FARMER

John B. Keane has introduced a new word into the English language — *chastitute*. This is the story of a chastitute, i.e. a man who has never lain down with a woman for reasons which are fully disclosed within this book. It is the tale of a lonely man who will not humble himself to achieve his heart's desire, whose need for female companionship whines and whimpers throughout. Here are the hilarious sex escapades of John Bosco McLane culminating finally in one dreadful deed.

IS THE HOLY GHOST REALLY A KERRYMAN

Is the Holy Ghost really a Kerryman? The obvious answer to this is: if he is not a Kerryman what is he? Is he just another ghost, a mere figment of the imagination like Hamlet's father, or is he something more sinister: a Corkman masquerading as a Kerryman or worse still a real Kerryman but having an inferiority complex; that is to say a Kerryman who thinks he's only the same as everybody else?

John B. Keane does not look upon those who peruse the pages of this book of his as mere readers. Far from it. He looks upon them, whether they be old or young, as students of the passing scene and not just the passing scene alone but as undergraduates in the university of things unusual.

Following the phenomenal success of John B. Keane's books, who can resist Keane on such varied topics as 'Wakes', 'Streaking', 'Epitaphs' and 'Long-Distance Talkers'? Nobody should miss reading this hilariously funny and entertaining book.

LETTERS OF A MATCHMAKER

These are the letters of a country matchmaker faithfully recorded by John B. Keane, whose knowledge of matchmaking is second to none.

In these letters is revealed the unquenchable, insatiable longing that smoulders unseen under the mute, impassive faces of our bachelor brethren.

Comparisons may be odious but readers will find it fascinating to contrast the Irish matchmaking system with that of the 'Cumangettum Love Parlour' in Philadelphia. They will meet many unique characters from the Judas Jennies of New York to Fionnuala Crust of Coomasahara who buried two giant-sized, sexless husbands but eventually found happiness with a pint-sized jockey from North Cork.

Send us your name and address if you would like to receive our complete catalogue of books

THE MERCIER PRESS LTD
4 Bridge Street, Cork,
Ireland.